OBSOLETE

Jessica Would Have Known
What to Say . . .

Todd cleared his throat. "Elizabeth, do you ever go bowling?"

Elizabeth closed her locker door and looked up. "Bowling? I've gone a few times with my family. Why?"

"Do you like it?"

"It's OK," Elizabeth said. "I'm pretty much of a klutz, though." She laughed, remembering the last time she had gone bowling. "I guess bowling is one of those things where you have to practice before you can be good at it."

"I guess," Todd agreed. Then after another long pause he said, "Well, see you around."

"See you around," she echoed, and Todd turned and walked away.

Why had Todd stopped to talk to her? Did he know it was her, or did he think at first that she was Jessica? Suddenly, Elizabeth could feel tears stinging the inside of her eyelids. Was bowling the kind of thing that Jessica had been talking about when she'd advised Elizabeth to find out what a boy was interested in and read up on it? Did Todd like bowling? If he did, Elizabeth was sure she had completely ruined any chance she had with him. She had even confessed how clumsy she was. How could she have said such a stupid thing? Todd Wilkins would never want to talk to her again!

SWEET VALLEY TWINS AND FRIENDS

Elizabeth's First Kiss

Written by
Jamie Suzanne

Created by
FRANCINE PASCAL

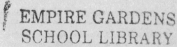

A BANTAM BOOK
NEW YORK · TORONTO · LONDON · SYDNEY · AUCKLAND

RL 4, 008–012

ELIZABETH'S FIRST KISS

A Bantam Book / November 1990

Sweet Valley High® and Sweet Valley Twins and Friends® are registered
trademarks of Francine Pascal.

Conceived by Francine Pascal

Produced by Daniel Weiss Associates, Inc.
33 West 17th Street
New York, NY 10011

Cover art by James Mathewuse

ISBN 0-553-15835-X

Published simultaneously in the United States and Canada

Bantam Books are published by Bantam Books, a division of Bantam Doubleday Dell
Publishing Group, Inc. Its trademark, consisting of the words "Bantam Books" and the
portrayal of a rooster, is Registered in U.S. Patent and Trademark Office and in other
countries. Marca Registrada. Bantam Books, 1540 Broadway, New York, New York 10036.

PRINTED IN THE UNITED STATES OF AMERICA

OPM   12   11   10   9

Elizabeth's First Kiss

One

◇

"Hi, Elizabeth!" Jessica Wakefield called to her twin as she dashed out through the doors of Sweet Valley Middle School.

"Hi, Jess," Elizabeth said with a smile. "Want to walk home with Amy and me?"

"I can't," Jessica said breathlessly as she caught up to them. "I have to wait for Lila. I just wondered if you'd seen Mary Wallace."

Elizabeth shook her head. "Not since lunch," she said. "Why?"

"Because," Jessica said importantly, "I have a message for her. From Peter Jeffries."

Amy looked curious. "What's the message?"

"The message is for *Mary*, and it's *private*," Jessica declared. Then she leaned forward and added, "But I'll tell you this much. Peter thinks Mary is *very* cute."

"If I see Mary, I'll tell her you're looking for her," Elizabeth said, shifting her backpack from one shoulder to the other.

"Thanks," Jessica replied. "By the way, Elizabeth, do you think you could help me with my math homework this weekend? I didn't understand anything in class today."

"Sure, Jess," Elizabeth said, "if you'll help me finish my art project."

Jessica grinned. "It's a deal. Oh, and Elizabeth, I just can't wait to tell you what happened today. I—" She glanced over her shoulder. "Oh, there's Lila. I've got to go." With a wave, Jessica dashed off to join her friend Lila Fowler.

"You know, Elizabeth," Amy said, "you're lucky to have a sister." She sighed. "Sometimes I wish I had one."

Elizabeth nodded. She felt lucky to have a sister, and she felt even luckier to have an identical twin. With their long, sun-streaked golden hair, sparkling blue-green eyes, and matching dimples in their left cheeks, Elizabeth and Jessica looked exactly alike. Sometimes, even their friends had a hard time telling them apart.

But even though they were identical on the

outside, the two girls had very different personalities. Jessica was a member of the Unicorns, an exclusive club consisting of the prettiest and most popular girls at school—and, in Elizabeth's opinion, the snobbiest. The topics discussed at Unicorn meetings usually ranged from the latest fashions and makeup ideas to the best party that month. But their all-time favorite topic was boys. Jessica could spend hours on the telephone with her fellow Unicorns talking about how adorable Denny Jacobson had looked in his new blue sweater, or wondering whether Rick Hunter had bumped into Ellen Riteman in the hall on purpose.

Elizabeth's interests were worlds apart from boys, clothes, and makeup. She was a serious and hard-working student and she hoped to be a writer some day. She dedicated much of her free time to writing and editing for the *Sweet Valley Sixers*, the class newspaper which she had helped found. Elizabeth loved to read and frequently set aside special time just to curl up with a good mystery novel. Most of all, she enjoyed spending time with her closest friends and she was always there for them if they needed her.

In spite of all their differences, the twins were

still best friends. They shared a special bond that only twins could understand.

"It *is* nice to have a sister," Elizabeth said. "And lately, it seems that we have even more to talk about."

Amy grinned and her eyes sparkled. "Like the big party that Aaron Dallas gave at the Hangout?" It had been the biggest, most important party ever, and everyone in the sixth grade was still talking about it.

"Or the trip to San Diego," Elizabeth added. She and Jessica had had a wonderful time together, visiting their cousin Robin. They'd experienced a lot together on that trip, and ever since they got back, they seemed to grow even closer.

At that moment, Elizabeth looked up and saw Todd Wilkins riding his bike. Elizabeth waved to him and Todd grinned shyly as he returned her wave.

"You know," Amy said thoughtfully, "Todd Wilkins is really cute."

Elizabeth felt herself blushing. She thought so too, although she felt shy about saying so. She had known Todd since kindergarten. But since fourth grade, she really hadn't seen much of him. In fact, she hadn't thought about him at all lately until she'd seen him at Aaron's party, dancing with Jessica. After that, she seemed to see him everywhere—at school, at the mall, even riding his bike through her neighborhood. And every time she saw him, butterflies would start fluttering away in her stomach and goosebumps would break out on her arms. Todd had grown a lot cuter since fourth grade. He had wavy brown hair and brown eyes framed by long lashes. Elizabeth had to admit that she was developing what her twin would call a major crush on him.

"Of course," Amy said, "Todd Wilkins isn't the only cute guy around. If you ask me, Ken is just as cute."

Amy and Ken Matthews had always been good friends, and recently Elizabeth had noticed the two of them spending more time together.

"Did I mention that Ken stopped by after Booster practice yesterday to show me his new bicycle?" Amy asked.

Elizabeth laughed. "Only twice," she said, thinking that this was probably the perfect time to tell Amy how she felt about Todd. But she wasn't sure she was ready to share her feelings. It was all new and strange and even a little scary. And anyway, she felt funny telling Amy something that she couldn't even share with Jessica—

and Elizabeth definitely knew she couldn't talk to her twin about Todd.

That was the problem. Elizabeth had the feeling that Jessica might be interested in Todd. Jessica had danced with him at Aaron's party, a fact that Caroline Pearce had mentioned in her last *Sixers* gossip column. It was clear to Elizabeth that Jessica enjoyed all of her classmates teasing her about him. Lately, his name came up in almost every conversation she had with her sister. Elizabeth decided that it wouldn't be right for her to like the same boy that her sister did. She couldn't tell anyone how she felt about Todd Wilkins.

"By the way," Jessica said to Lila as they headed home, "at lunch today, Todd asked me if I'd ever been bowling."

"He did?" Lila asked, giving Jessica an envious look. "Do you suppose he's going to ask you to go bowling with him?"

"Maybe," Jessica said.

"You are *so* lucky." Lila frowned and let out a big sigh.

Lila's father was one of the wealthier men in town, and Lila always got everything she wanted. Now, for the first time in her life, Jessica had something that Lila didn't—a boyfriend. Jessica was pleased at Lila's reaction.

"I never thought *you* would be the first of the sixth-grade Unicorns to have a real boyfriend," Lila went on.

"I'm sure that you'll be the next, Lila," Jessica said generously. "Didn't Jake Hamilton smile at you in the hall today?" Jake Hamilton was a handsome eighth grader, and one of the stars of the boys' basketball team. In Jessica's opinion, he wasn't as cute as Todd Wilkins, but he was very popular.

Lila nodded. "He did smile at me. And he is so cute, don't you think? Janet promised to tell him I think so." Janet Howell was the president of the Unicorn Club, and Lila's cousin. She was also in Jake's eighth-grade class. "You're right, Jessica," Lila decided. "I probably will be the next one to have a boyfriend."

When Jessica got home a few minutes later, the first thing she did was hurry to the kitchen to call Ellen Riteman, another fellow Unicorn. Ellen had been walking down the hall with Lila when Jake had smiled at her, and Jessica wanted to know what Ellen thought.

"Do you think Jake is really interested in Lila?" she asked.

"Maybe." Ellen sounded a little doubtful. "But I heard that he sat next to Roberta Manning when the eighth grade class took the bus to Santa Barbara for their field trip last week."

"That's too bad," Jessica said, secretly feeling pleased. "Lila really likes him."

"Don't tell her I told you," Ellen said quickly. "She'd be mad if she thought I was spreading gossip about Jake and somebody else."

"I won't," Jessica promised. "I wouldn't want to be the one to tell Lila—" She broke off. She had been gazing out the window and just then she spotted Todd Wilkins, riding his bike slowly down the street in front of her house.

"Jessica, are you there?" Ellen asked. "Jessica?"

"Ellen, you'll never guess who is riding his bicycle past my house right this very minute."

"Who?" Ellen asked excitedly.

"Todd Wilkins!" Jessica exclaimed. "He was over on the other side of the street but now he's on this side and he's riding *ve-ry* slowly. I can't believe it! He's looking this way. He's *definitely* looking at my house!"

"Wow, Jess," Ellen said. "Todd must really like you."

Jessica couldn't decide which was more fun— being around Todd or talking to her friends about him. It was great to be able to talk to her friends about him, especially since the idea of talking *to* him was still a little scary. What was even more exciting to Jessica was that she would be the first of all of her friends to have a boyfriend.

Recently, Jessica had been the only Unicorn who didn't have pierced ears. All of the other members had teased her about being treated like a baby by her parents. She had finally taken matters into her own hands and gotten her ears pierced. Now that she had a boyfriend, they really couldn't call her a baby.

"Hey, Jess," Ellen went on. "Did I tell you that Rick Hunter gave me part of his candy bar today after school?"

"Really?" Jessica said, feeling a little disappointed. Giving someone a candy bar was better than riding by on a bicycle.

"Uh-huh," Ellen said.

Jessica remembered that Todd Wilkins was much taller and much cuter than Rick, and brightened. "Well, I think that's a sign that he's interested, Ellen," she said graciously.

For the next five minutes, the girls traded stories about Todd and Rick. Finally, Jessica said good-bye and hung up the phone. She was looking out the window hoping to see Todd again, when the phone rang. She picked it up. "Hello."

"Hi. Is Stevie Wakefield there?" a girl said in a drawn-out Southern accent.

Jessica wrinkled her nose. *Stevie* Wakefield? "You must mean my brother, Steven," she said. Steven was fourteen and a freshman at Sweet Valley High. He'd been dating several girls for the past few months, but Jessica had never spoken to this one before.

"That's what I said," the girl replied, laughing. "Stevie Wakefield."

Jessica put down the receiver and yelled at the top of her lungs. "Ste-*ven*! There's some girl on the phone for you."

There was a clatter of footsteps in the hall, and a click on the line. "I've got it, Jess," Steven's voice said. "You can hang up the phone now."

"OK," Jessica said, and hung up the phone. Then she eased the receiver back off the hook. She just *had* to know who this girl was.

The girl was named Candice Stapleton. She was new at Sweet Valley High, and Steven had lent her his biology notebook. Candice was going on and on about how great Steven was.

"Oh, Stevie," Candice said with a sigh. "I can't tell you how much I appreciate your taking so much time to give me all this expert help. Why, I'd just be *lost* in Sweet Valley if you hadn't come along and rescued me. It's so wonderful to know I can count on you."

Jessica grimaced. How could Steven stand listening to this stuff?

Steven laughed, sounding pleased. "Oh, I haven't done anything—much," he added modestly.

Jessica smothered a giggle. Hastily, since Steven's conversation was coming to a close, she put the receiver back on the hook. She was getting a soda out of the refrigerator when Steven came into the kitchen and gave her a suspicious look.

"You *did* put that phone down when I told you to, didn't you?" he asked.

Jessica sighed. Whenever Steven got any kind of attention from a girl, it went straight to his head and he became even more annoying than usual.

"Of course I did," she said.

"I don't need any kid sisters listening in on my private telephone conversations," Steven warned her.

Jessica rolled her eyes. Steven was definitely going to be hard to live with for as long as this girlfriend lasted.

Two

◇

After dinner that night, Jessica was in her room, rummaging through heaps of clothes. She was trying to find something to wear to go shopping with some of the Unicorns the next day. She decided that she was either going to have to do her laundry or persuade Elizabeth to lend her something. But that would take some doing, since Elizabeth wasn't eager to loan clothes to her sister. Whatever she lent Jessica usually came back rumpled or stained. Jessica made a face, remembering the pretty yellow blouse that she had just plain lost. Maybe she should start with something less valuable, like socks, and work her way up.

Jessica found Elizabeth in her bedroom, curled

up on her bed with a magazine. She looked up when Jessica came in.

Jessica grinned at her twin. "Elizabeth, I can't find any clean socks in my room. Can I borrow your blue ones to wear tomorrow?"

"Sure." Elizabeth put her magazine down. "They're in the top drawer."

"Thanks," Jessica said, surprised that her twin had been so agreeable. She opened the dresser drawer and found it full of socks, all neatly rolled up in pairs. Jessica had never understood how Elizabeth managed to keep everything so well organized.

She pulled out the powder blue socks and then looked around the room thoughtfully. "Lizzie, didn't you just get a new blue T-shirt that matches these socks?" she asked.

"Uh-huh," Elizabeth replied. "It's in the third drawer. I haven't worn it yet. Do you want to borrow it?"

Jessica looked at her sister in amazement. She had expected to have to beg Elizabeth for the top. "Are you sure it's OK?"

"Yes. It's OK," Elizabeth reassured her. "Just take care of it, all right?"

"I will," Jessica promised happily. She opened

the drawer and quickly removed the T-shirt before Elizabeth could change her mind.

Elizabeth picked up the magazine again and began to leaf through the pages. "Hey, Jess," she said, "can I ask you something?"

Jessica sat down on the bed. "Sure, Elizabeth. What is it?"

Elizabeth put the magazine down, and Jessica noticed that it was one of her own teen fashion magazines—the kind that Elizabeth almost never read. Her twin usually preferred an Amanda Howard mystery or a book about horses.

"Well, I wanted to ask you about, uh, well, about boys."

"Boys?" Jessica thought she wasn't hearing her twin right. Elizabeth had never been interested in boys. In fact, Elizabeth had always made it clear that she thought Jessica spent far too much time worrying about boys. Now suddenly she was asking about them. Something strange was going on.

Jessica leaned forward eagerly. "What about boys? Any boy in particular?"

"No, not really," Elizabeth said, looking away. "I just wanted to know if you were, um, interested in somebody special . . ." She paused and started again, sounding flustered. "I mean, how would you go about getting him interested in you?"

Jessica bounced on the bed and grinned at her twin. "You mean you actually have a crush on someone? Elizabeth, that's great! Who is it? I can't give you any advice if I don't know who it is."

"Why?" Elizabeth asked.

"Because every boy is different and unique," Jessica explained patiently, repeating something she had read recently in a magazine article. "I mean, you wouldn't use the same, um"—Jessica thought about the exact way the magazine had phrased it—"the same *strategy* on every boy, would you?"

"Strategy?" Elizabeth asked uncertainly. She pulled her knees up under her chin and clasped her arms around her legs.

"Sure," Jessica said. "For example, a boy who's smart and shy, like Randy Mason, has different interests than somebody who's popular and good in sports, like Tom McKay. So you wouldn't act the same around them if you wanted them to be interested in you."

Elizabeth was looking terribly confused. "I don't know. Would I?"

Jessica laughed. She could hardly believe she was having a conversation about boys with her twin—a subject on which she was truly an expert. Not that she had a lot of personal experience, of course. She had gone out a few times with Josh Angler, a boy at Sweet Valley High, but that didn't really count because she had had to sneak out to do it. Her parents believed that she was too young to go out on a real date, but Jessica had read dozens of magazine articles and considered herself an authority on the topic.

"Of course you wouldn't, silly," she advised Elizabeth. "If you wanted to get Randy interested in you, you might buy one of those computer magazines he's always reading and impress him with how much you know about computers. If you were after Tom, you'd let him know that you're really crazy about basketball. Then you'd go and cheer at all the basketball games and congratulate him on all his great plays."

"But what if I still didn't know anything about computers even after I read the magazine?" Elizabeth asked. "Or what if I didn't happen to be crazy about basketball?"

"Then Randy or Tom probably wouldn't be interested in you," Jessica replied in a practical tone. "And the two of you wouldn't have anything to talk about when you were together. He'd be bored stiff."

"Oh," Elizabeth said. "That doesn't sound too great. I don't want to have to pretend I'm interested in something just to get a boy interested in me." She frowned.

"But that's the way it works, Elizabeth," Jessica replied. "It's really not that hard, and anyway, you have a lot of interests, so you might not have to pretend." She leaned forward. "Come on, Elizabeth, tell me who it is. Then we can figure out the best way to get him to like you."

Elizabeth looked at the floor. "Well, actually I'm not . . ." Her voice trailed off. Then she looked up and asked, "Who do *you* think would be a good choice for me, Jessica?"

"Well, all the Unicorns think Bruce Patman is really cute," Jessica said tentatively.

"You know I don't like Bruce, Jess," Elizabeth said.

"Then how about Aaron Dallas?" Jessica went on quickly. "He's cute, and he's pretty popular, especially after that great party he gave."

"Aaron's nice," Elizabeth replied, "but I don't like him any more than I used to just because he gave a good party."

"There's Tom McKay," Jessica said. "And Todd Wilkins."

Jessica noticed Elizabeth was blushing.

"I'm not interested in either of them," Elizabeth said, shaking her head. "Definitely *not* Todd Wilkins."

Jessica looked surprised. "Not even Todd? But he's really cute, Elizabeth, and he's also very nice. You guys were great friends in elementary school."

Elizabeth folded her arms. "I know, but we're not friends anymore. I barely know him now."

"Well, I think he's great," Jessica said. "If you promise not to tell, I'll tell you a secret, Lizzie." She paused.

"I promise," Elizabeth said.

Jessica lowered her voice confidentially. "I've got a *major* crush on Todd Wilkins."

Elizabeth swallowed. "You do?"

Jessica nodded. "And I think he likes me, too."

"What makes you think that?" Elizabeth asked, not able to look at her twin.

"Because he asked me to dance with him at Aaron's party," Jessica said promptly. "Ever since then, everybody's been teasing me about him. And there's that piece Caroline Pearce wrote about us in her gossip column."

"I know," Elizabeth said. "But that doesn't mean anything. People are teasing you because they read what Caroline wrote. That doesn't prove that Todd actually likes you."

Jessica stuck out her lower lip. "Well, I know he likes me," she retorted. "He's been watching me."

"Watching you?"

"That's right. I keep running into him every-where—at school, in the cafeteria, at the mall, at Casey's. I think Todd Wilkins might even be fol-lowing me around."

"Come on, Jess. Why would he do that?"

"I told you, because he likes me. Why else would he have been riding his bike past our house after school today?" Jessica asked. "I happened to be on the phone with Ellen and I looked out the window and there he was, riding by, staring at our house. And," she added, "Todd doesn't have any reason to be on this street, so that proves that he must have ridden over here just to see me." She gave Elizabeth a triumphant look.

"Well, yes, I guess," Elizabeth replied slowly. "I just thought maybe . . ."

"What?" Jessica asked. "What did you think?"

Elizabeth hesitated. "Nothing," she said after a moment.

Jessica stood up. "I'm really glad we had this talk, Elizabeth," she said happily. "I'm so excited that you're interested in boys now. You're finally catching up to me, even though you are the older one." She hugged Elizabeth's socks and T-shirt to her chest. "This is going to be great, Elizabeth. Now you'll understand how I feel about Todd."

"Todd makes you happy, I guess," Elizabeth said.

Jessica sighed. "Every time I think about him I get goosebumps all over, and the shivers, too. And I'm losing my appetite." It wasn't quite true, but she had read a book once where that was what had happened when the heroine fell in love.

Elizabeth shot her twin a skeptical look. "Really? You sure ate a lot at dinner tonight."

Jessica shrugged. "But that's because I didn't eat any ice cream after school today. And I only had one cookie at lunch." She turned to go.

"Hey, Jess," Elizabeth said. "Want to watch a movie on the VCR? I'll make some popcorn." She grinned. "Unless you don't have any appetite, that is."

Jessica grinned back. "Oh, I think I could eat a handful or two. But first I want to try on this top to see how it looks with my white pants."

"Go ahead," Elizabeth said. "I'll start the popcorn."

Jessica went to her room, and Elizabeth walked

slowly downstairs to the kitchen. She felt like watching a funny movie. She had to do something to cheer herself up now that she knew for certain that she and her twin liked the same boy. It sounded as if Todd liked Jessica, too. She sighed heavily as she plugged in the popcorn popper and dumped in the popcorn. She had to put Todd out of her mind. No matter what, she couldn't let Jessica know how she felt about him.

A moment later, Jessica came bounding into the kitchen. "The popcorn smells great. I'm starving," she said.

Then Steven came into the room through the back door. "All right! Popcorn!" he exclaimed. "How'd you guys know that's what we wanted?"

Jessica turned around. A pretty girl with curly strawberry blond hair and hazel eyes was standing beside Steven. Jessica looked at her with curiosity. She must be Candice, the girl who had called Steven that afternoon on the phone.

"We didn't know you wanted popcorn," Elizabeth was saying. "Jess and I were making it for ourselves. We're going to watch that movie Mom taped last week." She smiled at the girl. "I can make another batch for you, if you want."

"That's OK, we'll take this batch," Steven said over his shoulder, as he was getting two bowls out of the cupboard. "You guys can make more for yourselves. Lindsay and I are going to watch the ice hockey game." He gave the girl a smile. "With Mom and Dad out, we'll have the den to ourselves."

Jessica frowned. *Lindsay?* she thought. She could have sworn the girl on the phone had said her name was *Candice*.

Elizabeth was frowning, too. "But Jessica and I were just about to put on a movie, Steven," she objected.

"Come on, Liz," Steven said. "You can watch the movie anytime. This game is really important and we don't want to miss it."

"Since when have you become interested in ice hockey?" Jessica demanded. "I remember hearing you tell Dad you didn't even like it."

Steven turned bright red. "Well, it isn't that I don't like ice hockey, exactly. It's just that I—I mean—"

"I'm the one who's interested in ice hockey," Lindsay told Jessica. "I used to play on our junior high team back in Minnesota."

This definitely wasn't the girl who had told Steven how great he was over the phone this afternoon, Jessica was certain.

"Steven, I don't think it's fair for us to keep

your sisters from watching their movie," Lindsay went on. "Why don't we walk over to my house and watch the game there? Dad and Mom are sure to be watching it, anyway."

"It's OK, Lindsay," Steven said breezily. "The girls don't really mind." He gave Elizabeth a very pointed look. "Do you, Elizabeth?" It was obvious that he wanted to watch the game in the den, without any parents around.

But before Elizabeth could answer, Lindsay spoke again. "I'd much rather go to my house to watch the game," she said firmly. "You can come, too, Steven. But if you don't like ice hockey, please don't feel you have to." With that, she turned to leave.

Open-mouthed, Steven followed her.

The minute they had gone, Jessica burst out laughing. "Did you see the look on Steven's face when Lindsay took charge? I'll bet that's never happened to him before."

"He really got red when you said he didn't like ice hockey," Elizabeth said thoughtfully. "I guess he was pretending to like it just because Lindsay does."

"I guess," Jessica said. "Hey, I wonder if Steven is dating two girls." She told Elizabeth about the phone call from Candice, then started toward the den. "I'll go put the movie on."

"OK," Elizabeth replied. "I'll bring the popcorn and the drinks."

As Elizabeth fixed their tray, she thought about what had just happened. She could hardly believe that Steven was pretending to like ice hockey just to impress a girl. Well, at least this strategy business worked both ways. That was good news.

Three

◇

In the corner booth at Casey's Place, Lila, Ellen, Mary Wallace, and Jessica were digging into their sundaes. They had spent the morning shopping and decided it was definitely time for an ice cream stop.

"So, did you guys hear that Todd rode his bike by Jessica's house yesterday just to get a glimpse of her?" Ellen said.

"He did?" Lila asked.

Jessica nodded and smiled modestly.

"Wow, Jess. That's great," Mary said. "Do you like him?"

Jessica was about to tell Mary how she felt, but before she had a chance to say anything more about Todd, Ellen started talking about Rick Hunter and the candy bar he had given her.

"I don't know why everybody is suddenly so crazy about boys," Lila said crossly. "I mean, they're fine, but they're not *everything*. There's plenty of other stuff to talk about, like clothes and movies and music. Did you notice my new earrings, Jess?" She shook her head and her dangling silver earrings jingled softly.

"You're right, Lila," Jessica said, knowing her friend was feeling envious. "There are other things to talk about, but boys are the most fun. And everybody's interested in them now." She laughed. "Even Elizabeth."

Lila paused, her spoon halfway to her mouth. "*Your* sister's got a boyfriend? Oh, come on, Jessica, who are you trying to fool? Elizabeth's such a bookworm. She doesn't even know that boys exist."

Jessica took a mouthful of ice cream, feeling stung. She hated to hear anybody criticize her sister. "I wouldn't say that, Lila," Jessica snapped. "Elizabeth has a *lot* of interests that you don't know about."

"But everyone knows Elizabeth's interests have never included boys," Lila countered.

"Well, now they do," Jessica retorted. "Last

night she asked my advice about how to get a boy interested in her."

"What did you tell her?" Mary wanted to know. "I could use a little help, too."

"I told her that the first thing she should do is find out what he was interested in and study up on it," Jessica replied. "That way, she'd have something to talk to him about."

Ellen nodded. "Good advice," she said. "If Elizabeth listens to you, she may actually get somewhere with him, whoever he is."

"I doubt it," Lila said. "Elizabeth needs more than just advice on what to talk about. She could use some help with her appearance, too."

"What do you mean, Lila?" Jessica demanded hotly.

"Don't be so defensive, Jessica," Lila said. "You've got to admit that even though Elizabeth is your twin, she's not too fashion-conscious. In fact, most of the time, she dresses like she's back in elementary school."

"Lila's right, Jessica," Ellen agreed. "I mean, look at the way Elizabeth wears her hair. You curl yours and wear it down. Elizabeth always pulls hers back into a ponytail or puts barrettes in it like a little kid."

"And she wears those awful plaid blouses to

school," Lila went on, smoothing out her own expensive designer top.

"And she never wears any makeup," Ellen went on.

"Until she's willing to grow up a little," Lila concluded with a note of authority, "she'll never get a boy interested in her."

Jessica sighed. She could defend Elizabeth on a lot of things, but when it came to her twin's appearance, she had to admit that Lila and Ellen had a point. Even though the twins were identical, they had completely different taste in clothes. Elizabeth usually dressed much more conservatively than Jessica. Jessica had never really noticed that her twin dressed in a babyish style. After all, she frequently borrowed clothes from Elizabeth. But, now that she thought about it, maybe her friends were right.

"What Elizabeth needs is a makeover," Lila declared.

Of course, Jessica thought happily. *Why didn't I think of that?*

"That's a great idea, Lila," Ellen said. "Elizabeth could use a makeover."

"She would look nice if she wore her hair down more often," Mary agreed.

"But knowing Elizabeth," Lila went on, "I

doubt that she'll ever go to the trouble of making herself over."

"Oh, I don't know," Jessica found herself saying. "Maybe if I approached her in the right way. . . ."

Lila laughed. "I'd be totally shocked if she said yes, Jessica. I think you're wasting your time. She'll never give up that little-kid look."

Jessica frowned. What made Lila think she was always right?

Ellen finished the last of her sundae. "Hmmm. I wonder what boy she's interested in."

"Me too," Mary said. "Didn't she tell you, Jessica?"

Jessica shook her head. "No. She refuses to tell me." Somehow, she had to find a way to discover Elizabeth's secret.

"Ellen," Lila said, looking at her watch, "didn't we tell your mother to pick us up five minutes from now?"

Ellen pushed her glass away. "We'd better hurry," she said. She and Lila got up and hurried off.

Mary leaned back in the seat. "Isn't it nice to finally be growing up?" she asked in a dreamy voice. "I mean, to have boyfriends and all?"

Jessica nodded. She didn't want to tell Mary

the real reason it felt so good. She loved seeing Lila envy her for once.

Mary looked up. "Isn't that your brother?" she asked.

Jessica looked around. Steven had just come in and was ordering ice cream. A very pretty girl was standing beside him at the counter. She had long black hair, dark eyes, and the creamiest skin Jessica had ever seen.

"Who's that girl with him?" Mary asked curiously. "I don't think I've seen her around before. She's really pretty."

"I wonder if that's Candice," Jessica said. "Candice Stapleton," she explained to Mary. "She's one of Steven's girlfriends. She's from the South. At least, she's got a Southern accent."

At that moment, the two of them could hear the dark-haired girl's voice over the noise of the crowd.

"Oh, thank you, Stevie," she said, taking the banana split Steven handed her. They headed for a table on the other side of the room and sat down, pulling their chairs close together.

Jessica grinned. "That's Candice, all right," she said. "*Stev-ie*," she mimicked.

Mary laughed. "You said that she's *one* of

your brother's girlfriends?" she asked. "You mean, he has more than one?"

"Yeah. Can you believe it?" Jessica said. "He's got two. The other one is named Lindsay. She used to play ice hockey."

Mary's eyes widened. "Ice hockey? Really? I didn't know girls played ice hockey."

"Steven says she's a great athlete. Actually," Jessica confided, "I like Lindsay better. She doesn't let Steven push her around. And she doesn't call him *Stev-ie*."

"It looks like Steven is having a good time," Mary observed, looking at Steven and Candice. Candice was leaning toward Steven, looking up at him with her dark eyes. "If you ask me, Candice is a flirt."

"That's what I think, too," Jessica agreed. She watched Steven and Candice for a minute. "Steven's really loving the attention, isn't he?" she asked in disgust.

Mary shrugged. "Well, that's how some girls act around boys," she said. "I don't like it, but sometimes it seems to work. I mean, some boys are impressed by it."

Jessica pushed her empty bowl away and stood up. "Come on," she said. "Let's have some fun."

When she got to Steven's table, Jessica stopped, pretending to be surprised. "Why, *Stevie,*" she said, with a wicked grin, "I can't believe I bumped into you like this." She turned to Candice. "Don't you want to introduce me to your friend?"

With a dark look at Jessica, Steven mumbled, "Candice, this is my sister, Jessica. My baby sister."

Candice smiled graciously, showing beautiful white teeth. "It's so nice to meet you, Jessica," she said. Then, before Steven could stop her, she said, "Would you like to join us?"

"No," Steven said quickly. "I mean, I'm sure Jessica has other things to do. Like shopping, stuff like that."

"Well, I don't know," Jessica said, "maybe I could spare a few minutes." She turned to Mary. "What do you think, Mary? Do we have time for some more ice cream?" Steven was beginning to look panicked. "No, I don't think we *do* have the time, after all," she said. "Come on, Mary, we'd better get going."

She could almost hear Steven's sigh of relief when she and Mary walked away. Once out the door, Mary giggled.

"Poor Steven," she said. "You really scared

him. He thought for a minute that he was going to have to sit there with you *and* Candice."

Jessica grinned. "More than that," she said. "He thought that if I sat down I'd spill the beans about Lindsay."

Elizabeth had been trying to concentrate on her English homework on Sunday afternoon, but she couldn't stop thinking about Todd. The more she tried *not* to think about him, the more she thought about him. She knew that Jessica liked Todd, and it wasn't right for her to like somebody that her sister already liked.

But then it occurred to her that Jessica could change her mind at any minute. It would be just like Jessica to fall madly in love with a boy one day, and then give him up for some other cute boy the next day. If she did, Elizabeth thought, it might be a good idea to have a plan in mind to get Todd's attention.

Elizabeth and Todd had known each other for such a long time that he probably didn't even notice her anymore. Maybe what she needed was a different look to get his attention. She untied her ponytail and shook out her hair, trying to imagine how she could fix her hair so that she looked different, a bit more sophisticated.

At that moment, Jessica came through the door. "Hi, Elizabeth," she said. She stopped short, seeing her sister sitting at her desk with her hair down around her shoulders.

"Hi," Elizabeth said absently, running her hand through her hair. "Jess, do you think Mom would let me get a perm?"

Jessica looked surprised. "A *perm*?" she asked.

Elizabeth stood up and went to look at herself in the mirror.

"Well, I think it would be nice to have a little curl in my hair," she said. "Maybe if I got a perm, I would have some soft curls, like Sophia Rizzo. My hair is so *straight*. It's so boring."

"You don't need a perm," Jessica told her. "You could use a curling iron, the way I do. My hair's just as straight as yours, you know. Do you want me to show you how to use it?"

"Jess, that would be great!" Elizabeth exclaimed.

"While we're at it, I could show you a few makeup tricks, too. After all, if you're going to change your hair, you might as well try some other new looks."

Elizabeth smiled. "All right, Jess. But don't go overboard." She still wanted people, especially Todd, to be able to recognize her.

"I won't, Elizabeth. Don't worry." Jessica led her twin into the bathroom which connected their bedrooms.

"Hey, I have a great idea," Jessica said as a thought occurred to her. "How about if you lend me your new purple skirt in exchange for a beauty lesson?"

"OK, Jess," Elizabeth said, laughing.

"I think I'll wear it tomorrow with my lavender sweater. Thanks, Elizabeth." She plugged in the curling iron and began brushing her twin's hair. "Todd is going to love it," Jessica said, thinking of the admiring look that would cross his face when he saw her in that beautiful purple skirt.

Elizabeth whirled around, stifling a gasp. Sometimes she and her twin almost seemed to read each other's minds, but this was too much!

"Todd?" She swallowed. "You mean, Todd Wilkins? Jessica, I *told* you. I don't like Todd."

"Not you, silly," Jessica said. "I was just thinking about how much he'll like the skirt on me."

"Oh." Elizabeth was relieved. Jessica hadn't guessed, after all.

"And somebody else is going to be pleased, too," Jessica went on. "The boy you're trying to impress, I mean." She put down the brush and wrapped a strand of Elizabeth's hair around the curling iron. "Come on, Lizzie," she coaxed. "Aren't you going to tell me who it is? I promise I won't tell a soul. Your secret will be totally safe."

"Right, Jess," Elizabeth said, smiling and shaking her head. Her sister rarely kept secrets. "Anyway, I'm not telling anybody until I see if he likes me, too." She was glad to have an excuse not to tell Jessica.

"I can't believe you won't tell your only sister," Jessica said, pouting. "Won't you at least give me a hint?"

Elizabeth shook her head firmly.

For the next half hour, while Jessica showed her twin how to apply blush and lipstick, she named boy after boy in the sixth-grade class at Sweet Valley Middle School, and several from the seventh and eighth. But no matter how hard Jessica tried, Elizabeth wouldn't say one more word about boys.

When Jessica was finished, she stepped back to admire her work. "Well," she demanded, "what do you think?"

Elizabeth stared at herself in the mirror. She could hardly believe what she saw. Her silky blond hair fell in soft, shining curls around her shoulders. Her cheeks and lips glowed with a soft shade of pink.

"I look just like you," she said.

Jessica laughed. "Of course! We're identical twins."

"I mean, I look even more like you than usual," Elizabeth said. She picked up a hand mirror and turned so that she could see the golden waves of hair falling down her back.

"Don't you like it?" Jessica asked.

Elizabeth wasn't sure whether she liked it or not. The reflection in the mirror looked terrific, but it didn't seem like *her*. Still, she hated to say that to Jessica after all her hard work. "Of *course*! I love it, Jessica. Thank you," she fibbed.

"He'll like it, too," Jessica said wisely, "whoever he is."

Elizabeth looked at her twin in the mirror and laughed. "Forget it, Jess. I'm not telling you!"

"OK, OK," Jessica said with a defeated sigh. She headed back to her room. "Hey, Elizabeth, I got a new Darcy Campman tape yesterday," she called out. "Do you want to hear it?"

Elizabeth turned on the water and reached for the soap. "Sure," she said. "I really like Darcy Campman."

Jessica went to the bathroom door. "What are you doing?" she said in alarm.

Elizabeth turned around, her face covered with soapsuds. "I'm washing my face," she replied.

"But you're ruining my work!" Jessica wailed.

Elizabeth laughed. "I can put it back on, can't I?"

"I guess so," Jessica said. She started downstairs to get the tape that she had left on the coffee table in the living room.

In the hallway outside the den, Jessica hesitated. Lindsay had dropped in a little while ago, and Steven had come upstairs to announce that the two of them were going to work on a science project in the den and preferred not to be bothered.

But there was music coming from the den—music from Jessica's new tape. Carefully, she eased the door open a tiny crack and peeked in. Steven was dancing with Lindsay. Jessica closed the door carefully and started to go back upstairs. She was determined to report to Elizabeth all the details of what she had just witnessed. But, just as she reached the stairs, the phone rang. Jessica ran toward the kitchen, but Steven was faster than she was.

"Hello, Wakefield residence," Steven said.

"Oh, hi, Candice." Jessica stood still, straining to hear.

"I'd love to talk to you, Candice," he was saying. "But I . . . uh, I'm kind of busy right now."

Jessica grinned. *Busy?* she thought. *You bet. Busy dancing with another girl.*

"No, uh, nothing important," Steven said. Then he hastily corrected himself. "Well, ah, actually it *is* important. I, er, I'm doing something for my . . . my father. Something that I have to finish right away. So I, um, need to say good-bye." There was a pause. Then, in an even lower voice, Steven said, "Yes, you're very special to me, too, Candice." He cleared his throat. "I, ah, can't wait to see you tomorrow." Then he hung up.

When Steven came out of the kitchen, his face was red. It got even redder when he looked up and saw Jessica standing near the stairs.

"You were spying on me!" he shouted. And then, lowering his voice so that Lindsay wouldn't hear, he hissed, "You'd better not say a word about this, Jess."

"I don't know what you're talking about, Steven," Jessica said sweetly. "I was just on my way downstairs to get my Darcy Campman tape."

And as Steven glared at her, she turned and

ran upstairs, giggling. She couldn't wait to tell Elizabeth that their big brother had put himself right in the middle of a romantic triangle. He had not one, but *two* girlfriends!

Four

◇

On Monday morning, when Elizabeth got up, she decided to go to school looking just the same as always. But just as she was pulling on her jeans, Jessica came in. She was carrying a blue-and-green cotton dress in one hand and a curling iron in the other.

"I thought you might want to borrow this dress today," Jessica said. "And we've got plenty of time to do your hair."

"But I didn't . . . I mean . . ."

Jessica frowned. "I went to a lot of trouble helping you fix yourself up yesterday, Elizabeth. You're not going to let it go to waste, are you?"

By the time Elizabeth set off for school, she looked exactly as she had the day before: her hair fell in soft waves around her shoulders and she had on just a touch of pink blusher and lip gloss. Instead of her jeans, she had on Jessica's blue-and-green dress and her own new white sandals. Even though she knew that she looked great, she couldn't help feeling uncomfortable. The curls and the makeup and the clothes didn't seem right. She didn't feel like *herself*.

She must not have looked like herself, either. When she met Amy at the door of Mr. Davis's homeroom, her friend immediately mistook her for Jessica.

"Jessica," Amy said, "have you seen Elizabeth? I need to talk to her."

Elizabeth smiled shyly. "You're talking to her," she said.

"Come on, Jessica," Amy said impatiently. "You know that Elizabeth doesn't wear makeup. Besides, that's your dress!"

"It's me, Amy," Elizabeth insisted. "Jessica gave me a makeover and loaned me her dress."

Just as Elizabeth finally convinced Amy, Sophia Rizzo came along, and Elizabeth had to go through the makeover story all over again. But she didn't tell either of her friends why she had decided to curl her hair, put on makeup, and wear her twin's dress. When they asked, she just shrugged.

"I felt like doing it," was all she would say. "It was time for a change."

On the other side of the room, the Unicorns had noticed Elizabeth's new look, too.

"What a change!" Ellen exclaimed. "You did a great job, Jessica."

"Yes," Lila agreed, although she didn't sound very sincere. "You made her look just like you."

"How did you get her to listen to you?" Ellen asked.

"Actually," Jessica confessed, "she didn't argue with me at all. It was her idea. I told you, she's interested in a boy and she's trying to get him to notice her."

The Unicorns watched as Randy Mason, Ken Matthews, and Jim Sturbridge approached Elizabeth. With a feeling of satisfaction, Jessica saw that the boys were giving Elizabeth some admiring glances.

Lila frowned. "Well, Jessica, you seem to have accomplished your goal," she said in a sharp voice. "Which of the boys is she interested in?"

"I don't know," Jessica admitted. "I already told you, I couldn't get her to tell me."

"She still wouldn't tell you?" Ellen said. "What kind of a sister is she?"

"Really, Jessica," Lila said, shaking her head disapprovingly. "You're always going on and on about how great it is to have a twin, how you can tell each other everything."

"Well, usually we do," Jessica replied defensively. "But that doesn't mean we can't have secrets from each other."

"Well, if *I* had a sister, we wouldn't keep secrets." Lila sniffed. "Especially not about something as important as a boyfriend."

"I'll bet it's Jim Sturbridge," Ellen said in a gossipy tone.

"But Jim likes Billie Layton," Lila reminded Ellen. Billie was a Unicorn and also the star of the local little league team.

"Billie's still more interested in baseball than in boys," Ellen retorted. "Anyway, Jim is giving Elizabeth something. It looks like a note."

Jessica craned her neck for a look. Jim was handing a piece of paper to Elizabeth. Ellen was right. Elizabeth liked Jim Sturbridge.

Jessica was on her way to English when she decided to stop at the water fountain and get a drink. She was just turning to leave when she ran into Todd. He had on a blue shirt that made him look adorable.

"Hi, Todd," Jessica cooed. She smoothed down Elizabeth's purple skirt, feeling glad that she had worn it. She knew it looked fabulous on her.

"Uh, hi," Todd said. He blushed a little and gave her a shy smile. "How are things?"

"Just fine," Jessica said. She tossed her head, wishing that Lila and Ellen or even Caroline Pearce would walk by and see her talking to Todd. If Caroline saw them, everybody would know. Caroline was the biggest gossip in the sixth grade.

Todd grinned. "That's good." He looked down. "Uh, listen, Elizabeth, I was wondering if—"

Jessica frowned. "I'm not Elizabeth, Todd," she corrected him. "I'm Jessica."

Todd turned bright red. "Jessica? Oh, I'm sorry. I didn't mean—"

"That's all right, Todd," Jessica said sweetly. "People get us mixed up all the time. We look a lot alike."

"Yeah, you do," Todd said. He grinned. "You sure fooled me."

At that moment, Janet Howell walked by, with several of the eighth-grade Unicorns. When

Janet saw Jessica with Todd, she smiled. "Hi, Jessica," she said. She gave Todd an approving look. "Hello, Todd," she added.

"Who was that?" Todd asked, when she had gone.

"You don't know Janet Howell?" Jessica asked, surprised. "She's president of the Unicorns." She lifted her chin proudly. "I'm a Unicorn, too."

Todd nodded. "Is Elizabeth a Unicorn, too?"

"No," Jessica said. "Of course," she added hastily, "she could have been if she wanted to. The Unicorns asked her to join, but she said no." It was true, in a way. Jessica had gotten the Unicorns to ask Elizabeth to join. But Elizabeth had been bored by the meetings and had decided that she and the Unicorns didn't have anything in common.

Jessica frowned. Why were they spending so much time talking about Elizabeth? Then she smiled and casually leaned forward. "Wasn't that you I saw the other night, Todd? Riding your bike past my house?"

Todd nodded. "Yeah. I was on my way home from Jim Sturbridge's house."

Jessica waited, hoping he would say something more. But he didn't. He only said, "Well, it's been nice talking to you, Jessica. See you."

Then, with a quick wave of his hand, he was gone.

For a moment, Jessica stared after him, feeling disappointed. But then she shook the feeling off. Todd was pretty shy. She was confident that before too long, he was going to work up the nerve to tell her that he liked her. She smiled to herself. Luckily, Janet and some of the Unicorns had seen them talking together, and that was almost as good.

Jessica's crush on Todd was now all everyone was talking about at Sweet Valley Middle School. Everybody who had been at Aaron's party had seen them dancing together, and the seventh and eighth graders who hadn't been to the party had read about Jessica and Todd in Caroline Pearce's gossip column. It made Jessica feel very good that somebody as important as Janet Howell knew about her and Todd. When she ran into Janet in the cafeteria line with some of the other Unicorns, she wasn't at all surprised when Janet mentioned seeing the two of them together.

"Yes," Jessica said modestly, "it was really nice to bump into him unexpectedly like that."

"It didn't look to me as if he just came along

by accident," Janet said. "I'll bet he planned it to happen that way."

Jessica smiled. That was what she'd been thinking, too. It was just too much of a coincidence for the two of them to bump into each other, especially after he had ridden his bicycle right by her house.

Lila pushed impatiently between Jessica and Janet. "Have you talked to Jake Hamilton yet, Janet?" she asked. "Did you remember to mention me?"

"Of course I did, Lila," Janet replied.

"Well, what did he say?" Lila demanded.

Janet leaned forward and whispered in Lila's ear.

"What did he say? What did he say?" Ellen and Jessica begged when Janet had gone to join her friends at a table.

Lila gave them a look of smug self-importance. "Jake told Janet that he thought I was kind of cute and that he hopes to talk to me one of these days."

"Wow, Lila, that's great news!" Ellen gushed. "Just think, pretty soon we'll all have boyfriends."

Jessica didn't think what Jake had said sounded too promising, but she knew Lila wouldn't appreciate hearing that, especially from her. She paid for her lunch, then looked around the cafeteria for a free table. "Oh, there's Todd!" she said, spotting him at a table nearby.

Lila frowned. "You're always talking about Todd," she said crossly. "Why don't you *do* something about him for a change?"

Jessica shifted her tray. "Like what?" she asked uneasily.

"Well, for starters, you could go over and eat lunch with him," Lila said.

Jessica hesitated. When she really thought about it, she wasn't sure that Todd was interested in her. The meetings she had bragged about might have been coincidental. Even riding past her house might have been an accident. But she couldn't tell her friends that.

Ellen nodded. "Lila's right, Jessica. If Todd really likes you, he'll be happy to have lunch with you."

"Go on, Jessica," Lila prodded. When she noticed Jessica hesitating, she narrowed her eyes and said, "I *dare* you."

Jessica really didn't want to go over to Todd's table all by herself. But she couldn't turn down a dare, especially from Lila. If she did, it would look as if she had made up the whole romance.

"All right," she said. "I *will*."

Jessica marched across the cafeteria to the table where Todd was sitting with his friends Colin Harmon, Tom Sleeter, and Rick Hunter.

At Todd's table, she stood uncertainly for a moment beside an empty chair. Then Todd looked up and smiled at her.

"Hi, Elizabeth," he said. Then he corrected himself with a shake of his head. "I mean, Jessica. Sorry. I can't believe I made the same mistake again."

Jessica was glad the Unicorns couldn't hear what Todd had said. "That's OK, Todd. It's easy to mix us up, especially when we trade clothes."

"Oh, then that explains it," Todd said. "I always used to be able to tell you two apart." He moved his chair over a little. "Looking for somewhere to sit? This place is really crowded at lunchtime."

Jessica sat down, and Todd leaned toward her.

"Would you mind passing the salt, Jessica?" he asked.

Jessica handed him the salt, and her fingers accidentally brushed his. He smiled, and Jessica's heart beat faster. *Maybe if I bend my head a little toward his*, she thought, *Lila and Ellen will think we're having a deep conversation.*

But before Jessica could put her plan into action, Lila, Ellen, and Mary were crowding around the table, pulling up chairs and talking and flirting with the boys. In all the talk and laughter, Jessica and Todd didn't speak to each other for the rest of the lunch period. But Jessica didn't mind at all. The only thing that mattered to her was the fact that the two of them were sitting together, side by side, where everybody in the entire cafeteria could see them. When Todd and his friends got up from the table and went outside to throw a football around, she waved good-bye, smiling happily. It had been a very successful lunch, after all.

Five

◇

All through Mr. Nydick's history class that afternoon, Elizabeth felt totally miserable. At lunch, she and Amy and Sophia had been eating together when she'd spotted Jessica standing beside Todd's chair, giving him a confident smile. She had seen Jessica sit down next to Todd and begin chatting. A moment or two later, they had been surrounded by a group of laughing Unicorns and from then on she couldn't see what was happening between them.

But Elizabeth could imagine, and while Mr. Nydick talked about the Revolutionary War, Elizabeth was imagining the worst. It was obvious that Todd really did like Jessica. Elizabeth wished she were a little more like her twin. Jessica seemed to know exactly what to say and do around boys. She was obviously very comfortable with them.

Mr. Nydick turned on the slide projector and started to show some slides about George Washington and his army, lecturing as he went along. With a sigh, Elizabeth slid down in her seat and gave herself up to envy of the way her twin went about things.

Next to her in the darkened classroom, Colin Harmon was leaning closer.

"Elizabeth," he whispered, "did you get that last date Mr. Nydick mentioned?"

"Sorry," Elizabeth said. "I guess I missed it."

"That's OK," Colin whispered back. He grinned. "Hey, your hair looks different today."

Blushing, Elizabeth sat up straighter and tried to fix her eyes on Mr. Nydick's slide of Washington crossing the Potomac. But she couldn't keep her mind on what he was saying. She had the feeling that Colin meant his remark as a compliment, but it made her self-conscious. Ever since she had come into homeroom that morning, she had felt everybody looking at her. It had started when Randy and Ken and Jim Sturbridge had clustered around her in homeroom. Then, in science, Peter DeHaven had sat on her desk until the bell rang, asking her questions about that day's homework. She had wanted to attract attention, but the one boy whose attention she wanted hadn't even noticed her. He was too busy talking to her sister. Elizabeth kept reminding herself she shouldn't be thinking of Todd. The whole situation was horrible, but the worst thing about it was having no one to talk to.

Elizabeth was relieved when Mr. Nydick turned off the projector. She only had one more class before the day was over. As she was leaving the classroom, her twin caught up with her.

"Elizabeth," Jessica said, "I've been trying to talk to you all day."

"What is it, Jess?" she asked with a sinking feeling. She was afraid Jessica was going to ask her about her secret crush again.

"I want to tell you that I've got it all figured out," Jessica announced.

"Got what figured out?" Elizabeth asked, starting to walk ahead.

"The boy you like," Jessica said, hurrying to keep up.

Elizabeth held her breath. Had her twin really guessed? "Who do you think it is?" she asked.

Jessica leaned close and lowered her voice. "Jim Sturbridge. I saw you talking to him in homeroom this morning. I even saw him passing you a note. I'll bet it was a love note."

Elizabeth stopped walking. "A love note? That's ridiculous, Jess. Anyway, Billie Layton likes him, and I think he likes her. Jim and I were talking about the math homework, that's all."

"Really?" Jessica asked in disbelief.

"Ask Jim if you don't believe me," Elizabeth said with a shrug. Amy came up beside her. "Or ask Amy. She'll tell you."

"Ask me what?" Amy wanted to know.

Elizabeth turned to her. "Do you remember that paper I showed you in homeroom this morning?"

"You mean Jim Sturbridge's homework? What about it?"

Elizabeth cast a triumphant look at Jessica, who was frowning.

"So it isn't Jim," Jessica stated.

Elizabeth shook her head firmly.

"Well, then," Jessica demanded crossly, "who is it? And why won't you *tell* me? Why is it such a secret?"

"What are you guys talking about?" Amy asked, puzzled. She glanced from one twin to the other. "Who's got a secret?"

"Elizabeth has a secret crush on some boy,"

Jessica explained, "and she won't tell anybody who he is." She was starting to lose her patience.

Amy's eyes widened. "Elizabeth! Is that why you're so dressed up today?"

Elizabeth could feel her face getting red. She couldn't think of anything to say.

"I still think it's Jim Sturbridge," Jessica persisted, trying one more time to discover Elizabeth's secret.

Amy crossed her arms. "Maybe she just doesn't feel like telling you, Jessica," she defended Elizabeth. "She's got a right to keep it to herself if she wants to."

"Well, she *ought* to tell me," Jessica said huffily. "I helped her make herself over so she could impress him. I think she owes it to me to tell me who he is."

Elizabeth remained silent, and after a minute, Jessica walked off, looking angry. She was relieved she had gotten out of that sticky conversation, but she had to remind herself that it was with Amy's help. Jessica was just going to keep trying to figure out who she had a crush on. And now, Amy knew that she liked somebody, too.

"Listen, Elizabeth," Amy said, "if you want to tell me who you like, I promise not to tell anyone. But if you don't want to tell me, I promise I won't bother you about it either."

Elizabeth smiled. "Thanks, Amy," she said gratefully. "I just wish this whole thing weren't so complicated." She looked down at the dress Jessica had loaned her. "It's my own fault, really. I wish I hadn't let Jessica do my hair like this. I'm not even sure why I did it."

"You did it because you wanted to look your best," Amy said reassuringly. "There's nothing wrong with that." She hesitated. "Of course, I happen to think that you look best in your own clothes, but I really do like your hair the way it is now. And I have to admit that a little makeup looks good on you."

Elizabeth gave her friend a sideways glance. "Really, Amy?"

"Really." Amy nodded. "Maybe you can teach me how to use some, too." She laughed. "So Jessica thought you liked Jim Sturbridge, huh?"

"Yes," Elizabeth said. "But I don't, Amy."

"I believe you," Amy replied. "I think Jessica does, too."

When Jessica told Lila and Ellen what Elizabeth had said, they disagreed about it.

"If it isn't Jim," Ellen said thoughtfully, "it might be Colin Harmon. I saw him talking to her in history class."

"Well, Elizabeth can deny it all she wants, but I think it's Jim Sturbridge," Lila replied. She looked at Jessica. "What do you think?"

"I don't know what to think," Jessica admitted.

"If it isn't Colin Harmon," Ellen said, "maybe it's Randy Mason."

Lila laughed. "Randy Mason? He's so skinny and funny-looking. Even Elizabeth wouldn't be interested in Randy Mason." Suddenly she paused. There was a glint in her eye and her lips began to curve up into a smile.

"Lila," Ellen asked, "what are you thinking?"

Lila tilted her head to one side.

"Lila, are you scheming about my sister?" Jessica asked.

Lila's brown eyes sparkled. "It's just a harmless little prank," she said. "And it's funny! Even Elizabeth will think so. And nobody will get hurt, I promise." Lila put her hand over the silver unicorn pin she was wearing on her blouse. "Unicorn's honor."

Jessica narrowed her eyes. "What have you got in mind?" she asked suspiciously.

"You'll love it, Jessica," Lila said. She leaned

forward. "We'll let all the boys know that Elizabeth's looking for a boyfriend."

"What's so funny about that?" Ellen asked.

"Elizabeth will have more boyfriends than she can handle," Lila answered.

That afternoon, Elizabeth stayed after school to work on the next edition of the *Sixers*, which was due out in just a few days. She had finished her work and was getting her homework out of her locker when she looked up and saw Todd Wilkins walking down the empty hallway toward her. Her heart started pounding. Todd was wearing a red sweatshirt and his brown hair was slightly damp. A pair of basketball shoes were slung over his shoulder.

Elizabeth couldn't believe it when Todd stopped at her locker.

"Hi," he said, and then he paused and looked closer. "Elizabeth," he added. There seemed to be the tiniest hint of doubt in his voice.

"Hi, Todd," Elizabeth answered, as calmly as she could. Maybe he had only stopped because he thought she was Jessica. She reached for her English book, trying to think of what to say.

Todd shifted from one foot to the other. "I

guess you stayed after school today, huh?" he asked finally.

Elizabeth put her English book and her math book into her backpack. "Yes," she said, zipping up the bag. "I stayed to work on the paper."

She wanted to say more, but her tongue felt stuck to the roof of her mouth, and that was all she could manage.

There was a long pause while Elizabeth felt her cheeks getting pink. It was Todd's turn to talk, but if he didn't say anything, should she?

Finally Todd spoke up. "Me, too. I, uh, I mean, I stayed after school for basketball practice." He paused again. "Elizabeth, do you ever go bowling?"

Elizabeth closed her locker door and looked up. "Bowling? I've gone a few times with my family. Why?"

"Do you like it?"

"It's OK," Elizabeth said, slinging her backpack over her shoulder. "I'm pretty much of a klutz, though." She laughed, remembering the last time she had gone bowling. "My balls usually end up in the gutter. I guess bowling is one of those things you have to practice before you can be good at it."

"I guess," Todd agreed. Then, after another long pause he said, "Well, see you around."

"See you around," she echoed, and Todd turned and walked away.

Why had Todd stopped to talk to her? Did he know it was her, or did he think at first that she was Jessica? After all, she was wearing her sister's dress, and lots of kids had been confused that day about which twin was which.

Suddenly Elizabeth could feel tears stinging her eyelids. She couldn't pretend that it had been a good conversation. It had been a *horrible* conversation. They had stumbled around without anything really interesting to say. Why, for instance, had he asked her about bowling, of all things?

Then a thought struck her. Was bowling the kind of thing that Jessica had been talking about when she'd advised Elizabeth to find out what a boy was interested in? Did Todd like bowling? If he did, Elizabeth was sure she had completely ruined any chance she had with him. She had even confessed how clumsy she was. How could she have said such a stupid thing to somebody who obviously liked bowling and was probably very good at it? She had made a terrible mess of the entire conversation! Todd Wilkins would never want to talk to her again.

Elizabeth was still standing in the hallway when Amy came up behind her.

"On your way home?" Amy asked.

Wordlessly, Elizabeth nodded and the two girls walked out the door and onto the street.

"What's the matter, Elizabeth?" Amy asked. "You look weird. Is everything all right?"

"Yes," Elizabeth managed to say. She wanted to tell Amy what had happened, but she couldn't.

"Hey," Amy went on. "Did you hear about the new bowling alley in the mall? Some of the kids are talking about going bowling sometime soon."

"Really?" Elizabeth asked. Todd must have heard about the bowling alley, too.

Amy nodded, her eyes sparkling. "I think it sounds like fun, don't you? I like to bowl."

Elizabeth sighed, thinking about the mess she had made of her conversation with Todd. "It's OK," she said, as they crossed the street.

When they were almost at the Wakefield house, Amy pointed ahead. "Look, Elizabeth. There's Steven," she said.

Elizabeth looked in the direction Amy was pointing. Steven was walking his bike about a half block ahead of them. Beside him was a girl with long black hair.

"That must be Candice," Elizabeth said.

"Is she Steven's girlfriend?" Amy asked.

"Well, I'm not sure," Elizabeth replied. "She's been calling him a lot. But he's also friendly with a girl named Lindsay."

Amy raised her eyebrows. "Two girlfriends? I'll bet that's interesting."

Elizabeth laughed a little. "I'll bet it's a little complicated, too," she said.

Six

◇

Late that afternoon, Elizabeth was setting the table for dinner when she heard Steven on the telephone in the kitchen. He was talking to Lindsay, and something he said caught her attention.

"I was wondering if you'd like to go bowling on Saturday night. A great new alley just opened at the mall."

Jessica came into the dining room carrying a bowl of salad. "I've heard about that bowling alley," she said to Elizabeth. "Lila says that a lot of seventh and eighth graders are going there."

"Well, if you can't do it on Saturday, how about Friday?" the girls heard Steven say. Lindsay must have agreed, because he exclaimed, "Hey, terrific! See you then."

"Got a date with Lindsay for Friday?" Jessica asked innocently as Steven passed airily through the dining room. "What will Candice think of that?"

Steven glared at her, his good mood spoiled. "It's none of your business," he growled.

"Have you been to the new bowling alley yet?" Elizabeth asked Steven.

"No, it's only been open for a couple of weeks," Steven told her. "But a lot of the kids are interested in bowling, and maybe even starting a league." He was heading for the stairs when Mr. Wakefield came in from the backyard with a big platter of hamburgers he had just barbecued.

"Dinner's ready, everyone," Mr. Wakefield called.

"I know Todd likes to bowl," Jessica remarked. "He and Aaron Dallas were talking about going at lunch today. Elizabeth, maybe we should go to the bowling alley on Friday. We might run into him there."

Elizabeth was thinking. Maybe it wouldn't be a bad idea for her to improve her bowling. And Jessica was right. They might see Todd—although Elizabeth wasn't sure that she wanted to be around when Jessica and Todd were together.

Then a thought struck her. If she ran into

Todd at the bowling alley, would he remember that he had mentioned bowling to her and think that she had come there on purpose, just to see him? He might think it was a little strange, since she hadn't been very enthusiastic about bowling when he'd asked her about it. Just then another thought occurred to her. What if Todd had actually wanted to invite her to go bowling that afternoon? If he did want to ask her, she had ruined everything by telling him that she was a terrible bowler.

"Well, will you, Elizabeth?" Jessica begged. "Will you go bowling with me on Friday? It would be fun for the two of us to go together, don't you think?"

"I guess so," Elizabeth replied. She didn't really want to, but she couldn't think of a good excuse to tell her twin.

When they sat down to dinner, Elizabeth was still puzzling over her problem. Steven was helping himself to his third hamburger when the phone rang.

"I'll get it," Jessica cried, jumping up. "It's probably for me."

"No, I'll get it," Steven said. He was by the phone in a flash. Jessica didn't even have a chance.

"Whoever it is," Mrs. Wakefield said, raising her voice, "tell them to call back after dinner."

Steven was standing right outside the doorway to the kitchen and Elizabeth couldn't help overhearing his phone conversation. It was Candice. Elizabeth smothered a smile, remembering what Jessica had told her about the last time Candice had called, the day that Steven was entertaining Lindsay. Clearly, Steven had a problem.

"I don't think I can do it on Friday night, Candice," Steven was mumbling. "I have to do something . . . uh, with the family."

Jessica poked Elizabeth in the side and grinned. They both knew that Steven wasn't doing anything with the family on Friday night. He had asked Lindsay to go bowling with him!

Mr. Wakefield put down his fork. "Steven," Mr. Wakefield called loudly, "please excuse yourself and come back here and finish your dinner. You can talk on the phone after dinner."

"Listen, Candice," Steven said hurriedly, "I have to go. We're eating dinner." There was a pause. "Saturday night? Sure. We'll go to the movies. See you then." He didn't sound too excited about his date with Candice. He came back to the dinner table and was silent through the rest of the meal.

After dinner, Elizabeth and Jessica were getting ready to do the dishes. Steven was clearing the table with a scowl on his face. When he set down the last plate, Jessica started to tease him. "What's the matter, Steven? You don't look very happy for someone who's got two dates this weekend with two different girls. How lucky can you get?"

Steven growled something incomprehensible.

Jessica shook her head, pretending to be sympathetic. "I just wonder," she said thoughtfully, "what Candice would say if she found out that you're going out with Lindsay too."

Steven glared at Jessica, then shook his head and left the room. Obviously he was upset, and Elizabeth couldn't help feeling sorry for him. He had gotten himself into an awful mess, and Elizabeth didn't think it was fair for Jessica to be making it worse. She was just discovering herself how complicated love really was.

"I think it would be great to go bowling Friday night," Jessica said when Steven was gone. "Maybe we could even be on a team with Todd."

For the next ten minutes, Jessica didn't stop talking about Todd. She told Elizabeth how he had smiled at her at the water fountain that morning, and she recounted the conversation they'd had at lunch that day, word for word.

"Lila is so jealous that I have a boyfriend," Jessica confided. "Poor Lila can't even get Jake to say hello to her. I think Jake might be interested in Roberta Manning. After all, he never spends any time with Lila, not the way Todd does with me."

Elizabeth put the last dish into the dishwasher. Jessica had been talking nonstop about the attention Todd was paying to her. But as far as Elizabeth could tell, except for lunch that day, Jessica had hardly spent any time at all with Todd. Elizabeth was beginning to suspect that what Jessica liked even more than Todd was the attention she got from her friends for being the first of the sixth-grade Unicorns to have a boyfriend.

"Jessica," she said suddenly, "do you really like Todd?"

Jessica stared at her twin. "Of course," she said. "Isn't that what I've been telling you? I mean, everybody thinks he's so cute. Even Janet Howell, and she's an eighth grader."

Elizabeth felt a little hopeful. It certainly sounded as if Jessica liked the idea of having a boyfriend much more than she actually liked her boyfriend. If that were true, Elizabeth could feel free to like Todd herself, without worrying about her twin.

Jessica continued to rattle on about Todd, and Elizabeth grew more uncomfortable as the minutes went by. Jessica didn't sound even slightly interested in him. Then Jessica started to talk about Elizabeth's secret crush. "You can say whatever you want, Elizabeth, but I *still* think you like Jim Sturbridge."

Elizabeth couldn't take it any longer. "Who I like or don't like is none of your business, Jessica!" she shouted. She slammed the door of the dishwasher so hard that the dishes rattled. "I am tired of hearing about you and the Unicorns and your boyfriends. Can't you see I'm not interested?" She stormed out of the kitchen and ran all the way up to her room.

"I wonder what her problem is?" Jessica said out loud, and shrugged. She didn't mind if Elizabeth didn't want to hear about Todd, since she had plenty of friends who were willing to listen to her. They liked talking about boys, and they didn't keep any secrets from one another when it came to crushes. In fact, it was just the other way around. The Unicorns told one another everything, down to the very tiniest detail.

*   *   *

"Rick Hunter sat right in front of me during assembly this morning," Ellen bragged at lunch on Tuesday. "He kept turning around to look at me."

"Well, Peter Jeffries walked me home from school yesterday," Mary Wallace said.

All the girls gasped.

"Where's Todd today, Jessica?" Ellen asked, looking around. "How come you're not having lunch with him?"

"He had something important to do during lunch today," Jessica said. She wished she could tell them exactly what it was, but she couldn't. The truth was that she'd looked around for him when she came into the cafeteria and hadn't seen him anywhere, so she had decided that he must be doing something important. "I did talk to him this morning before math class, though," she added.

Not to be outdone, Lila put her elbows on the table and leaned forward. "Well, *I* got a note from Jake today," she announced.

All eyes were immediately turned from Jessica to Lila.

"What did it say?" Ellen asked excitedly. Lila smiled. "It said, 'yes,' " she replied. "And it was signed, 'Jake.' " She took it out of her purse. "Do you want to see it?" When the girls nodded their heads, she passed it around. Jessica took it, wishing that Todd had written her a note.

"What does it mean?" Ellen wanted to know. "Yes to what?"

"I wrote him a note and asked if he was going to basketball practice this afternoon," Lila explained. "Janet delivered it to him. 'Yes' means that he is."

"He must want you to come and watch him," Ellen said.

Lila nodded. "I'm sure that's what it means." She turned to Ellen and Jessica. "Would you like to go with me to watch the boys play basketball after school?"

"Sure," Ellen agreed. "Rick's on the team, too, so he'll be there."

"I'll go if Todd will be there," Jessica said. Privately, she was thinking that Lila's one-word note from Jake wasn't such a big deal. But she didn't want to embarrass Lila by saying so, especially when everybody else was acting like it was so exciting.

"I'm sure you'll want to save this," Ellen said, handing the note back to Lila.

"I'm going to put it in my scrapbook," Lila announced. "Along with my picture of Jake."

Jessica thought that was a good idea. She had a scrapbook, too. She could start collecting things from Todd. She could put in the picture of him that had appeared in the *Sixers* a few weeks ago.

After school, Jessica, Lila, and Ellen went to the gym to watch the boys play basketball. Todd didn't get there right away, and Jessica sat impatiently while Lila and Ellen clapped and cheered at every successful shot Jake and Rick made. After a little while, she stood up.

"I'm going," she said. "This isn't any fun."

"But it is!" Ellen objected. "Didn't you just see that basket Rick made?"

"You can't go. Here comes Todd," Lila said, pulling at Jessica's arm.

Jessica quickly sat back down.

Todd ran onto the court to join Rick and Jake. Within three minutes, he had sunk two baskets.

"Yay, Todd!" Jessica cried, clapping her hands and feeling very proud.

When practice was over, the girls walked home together, talking about the boys the whole time. Ellen and Lila had kept track of the baskets Rick and Jake had made.

"Rick made the most," Ellen bragged. "He made nine baskets."

"But Jake is very good on defense," Lila pointed out. "He kept the other team from scoring."

"How many baskets did Todd make?" Ellen asked.

"Just six," Jessica said. "But," she added, "he didn't play for that long."

When they reached the intersection where they had to split up, the girls said good-bye and walked off in different directions.

Jessica was still thinking about Todd when she got home. Elizabeth and Mrs. Wakefield were in the kitchen getting dinner ready.

"Hi, Jess. How about peeling some potatoes?" Mrs. Wakefield asked, giving Jessica a kiss. "How was school today?"

"School was great today!" Jessica exclaimed, happy to have a chance to talk some more about Todd. If Elizabeth didn't want to hear, she would have to leave the room.

"That's nice, dear," Mrs. Wakefield said. "I don't usually hear you sounding so enthusiastic about school."

Jessica sat down at the counter and began to peel potatoes. She told her mother about eating lunch with Todd the day before, and about watching him play basketball that afternoon.

"Oh, I see. So it's not your classes you're excited about after all," Mrs. Wakefield said, laughing.

Just then, Steven came in the back door and dropped his books on the counter. He grabbed an orange from the bowl on the table and headed for the hall.

"Not so fast, Steven," Mrs. Wakefield said. "I need you to get on your bike and go to the store for a few things. There's a list beside the phone. And a girl named Candice Stapleton called a few minutes ago. She wanted you to call her back."

Steven turned. "I don't suppose there was a call from Lindsay, was there?" he asked hopefully.

"No, just Candice," Mrs. Wakefield said.

Looking disappointed, Steven put the orange back in the bowl and went to the phone to pick up the list.

"The grocery store can wait a few minutes, Steven, if you want to make your phone call first," Mrs. Wakefield said.

"Oh, that's OK," Steven muttered. "I might as well get the groceries out of the way."

Jessica giggled. "Poor Steven," she said. "He's got one too many girlfriends."

"Jess," her mother said sharply, "don't make fun of your brother."

"Yeah, Jess," Steven said, "what makes you an expert, anyhow?" He grabbed the list and stomped out the door.

Seven

◇

"You dropped this," Amy said. It was Wednesday morning and Amy had just come by to meet Elizabeth before homeroom. She picked up a piece of paper off the floor in front of Elizabeth's locker. "It looks like a note from somebody."

Elizabeth looked at it. "How did a note get into my locker?" she wondered out loud.

"Sometimes people put notes through the vents," Amy said. "Who's it from?"

When Elizabeth unfolded the paper, she read, "You look really pretty with your hair curled." The note was signed, "Your Secret Admirer."

"Wow. I wonder who your secret admirer is?" Amy said. "Any ideas?"

"No, I can't guess," Elizabeth said, feeling

her face turn red. The day before, she had gone back to wearing her own clothes and no makeup, although she had left her hair curly. But lots of boys in her class continued to pay more attention to her than usual and she couldn't figure out what was going on. No one had ever left a note in her locker before.

Elizabeth sneaked a look around her at the kids who were standing in the hallway. Was somebody watching her to see how she responded when she found the note? Feeling very self-conscious, she folded it up and put it in her notebook, then headed for homeroom with Amy.

The same sort of thing happened several times that day. In English class, Mr. Bowman told everybody to team up with another person on the oral projects they were doing, and at least four different boys wanted to be Elizabeth's partner. She ended up with Winston Egbert. At lunch, Peter DeHaven put an ice cream sandwich on her tray. She tried to give it back, but he wouldn't take it.

When Elizabeth and her friends sat down at a table, Sophia Rizzo said, "I think it's your new look that's attracting all the attention."

"But I don't look that different," Elizabeth insisted. "All I did was change my hairstyle."

"I don't think it's got anything to do with the way you look, Elizabeth," Amy said, opening her carton of milk. "It just seems that everybody's thinking about romance. Ever since Aaron's party, love is in the air." She leaned forward and lowered her voice. "I just saw Mary Wallace holding hands with Peter Jeffries."

Sophia giggled. "Maybe love is like the measles," she suggested. "It's catching."

"Well, if that's the case," Amy said, laughing, "I hope Ken will catch it too." She clasped her hands over her heart and sighed dramatically. "Maybe we'll get stuck in quarantine together!"

Julie Porter and Elizabeth laughed.

Julie shook her head. "I don't see how anybody has any time for romance. Between getting my homework done and practicing my flute, I don't have a minute." Julie was an expert flutist and a member of the school orchestra.

Elizabeth nodded. She didn't have a lot of time for boys, either, considering the hours she spent working on the newspaper and doing her homework. But there was one particular boy that she would *make* time for, if she had the chance.

But she wasn't going to have the chance, she reminded herself sadly. If there had been any hope at all, she had ruined it yesterday, when she'd made such a terrible mess of their conversation. As if to prove the point, she looked across the cafeteria to see Jessica standing beside Todd. A second later, he had moved over and she was sitting down and smiling up at him.

Elizabeth was alone in the English classroom, after school, polishing up her latest article for the *Sweet Valley Sixers* when Caroline Pearce came in to deliver her gossip column. Elizabeth skimmed it quickly. Every single one of the items was about a girl-boy couple, and most of them were about Unicorns. There was one about Lila Fowler and Jake Hamilton, another about Mary Wallace and Peter Jeffries, and a third one about Jessica and Todd.

Elizabeth looked up. "Caroline," she said, "couldn't you find anything to write about besides the Unicorns' romances?"

Caroline pushed back her long red hair. "But Elizabeth," she said, "everybody's talking about romance. That's what they want to read about."

Elizabeth sighed. "Maybe. But I still think there ought to be something else in the column. Why don't you put in the news about Lisa Rainish getting that big part in the play? Or the football tickets that Ken Matthews won in the radio contest?"

Caroline made a face. "Those things aren't nearly as interesting to read about," she replied.

Elizabeth pushed the column back across the table. "All I'm saying is that romance isn't everything."

"Fine." Caroline snatched up the column and marched out the door, bumping into Amy.

"What's Caroline so mad about?" Amy asked as she slipped into a seat beside Elizabeth.

"We had a disagreement over how much romance she ought to put in her column," Elizabeth said.

"Speaking of romance, I think there's something you ought to know," Amy said.

Elizabeth glanced at her. Amy looked uncomfortable. "What's that?"

"Well, I just heard that a few of the Unicorns are spreading a rumor about you."

"A rumor!" Elizabeth exclaimed, sitting up straight. "What kind of rumor?"

"Maybe I shouldn't have mentioned it," Amy said unhappily.

"Amy," Elizabeth said, "just tell me."

"All right." Amy sighed uneasily. "But you're not going to like it. The Unicorns are spreading it around that you are looking for a boyfriend. They're saying that's why you borrowed your sister's clothes and put on makeup and fixed your hair."

"Looking for a boyfriend!" Elizabeth repeated, in a horrified voice. "This must have been Jessica's idea."

Amy nodded, looking miserable. "I just bumped into Julie on her way out of orchestra practice. She told me she heard it from her sister Johanna. Johanna's friends with some of the seventh-grade Unicorns. But I'm sure people won't actually believe the rumor, Elizabeth," she added hastily. "At least, not people who know you."

"But they already believe it," Elizabeth said hopelessly.

"How do you know?"

"Why else would somebody put a note in my locker and sign it 'Secret Admirer'?" Elizabeth demanded. "Why else would Winston Egbert run across the room to ask me to do the English project with him? Why else would Peter DeHaven give me an ice cream sandwich? The Unicorns' rumor accounts for all the attention I've been getting lately."

"Oh, Elizabeth," Amy breathed.

"I'm sure that those boys heard the rumor," Elizabeth said, blinking back tears. "And they saw the evidence—after all, I did get all dressed up on Monday, and I'm still curling my hair." She swallowed hard. "But not for long!" She grabbed a rubber band off a pile of papers in front of her and pulled her hair back into a ponytail.

Amy looked at her. "I like it better down, Elizabeth."

"So do I," Elizabeth said. "But it's humiliating for people to think I'm only wearing it that way because I'm looking for a boyfriend. How could Jessica say such an awful thing!"

Then another question came into Elizabeth's mind. What if Todd heard the rumor that she had changed her looks in order to try and get a boyfriend? What would he think of her?

That same afternoon, after school, Jessica, Lila, and Ellen went shopping in the mall. They had stopped at Casey's Place for ice cream. They were sipping milk shakes and discussing boys when suddenly Ellen nudged Jessica.

"There they are," she whispered excitedly. "They just came in!"

"Who?" Lila wanted to know. Her back was toward the door.

"Don't turn around!" Ellen exclaimed. "Don't act like you notice them."

Lila frowned. "Ellen," she said distinctly, "notice *who*?"

"It's Todd," Jessica whispered to Lila. "Rick and Jake are with him."

Lila fluffed up her brown hair. "Why didn't you say so?" she asked, straightening up. "What are they doing?"

"They're ordering sodas," Ellen reported.

"Now they're paying for them," Jessica said, after a minute.

"They're sitting down at a table up front," Ellen said, after another minute. She sounded disappointed. "I guess they didn't see us."

Jessica waved and smiled. "Yes, they did," she said. "But they're going to that other table anyway." She was disappointed too. She had hoped that Todd would come over and sit with her.

"That settles it," Lila said, finishing off the last of her milk shake. "Come on."

"Where?" Ellen asked.

"Jessica is going to talk to Todd," Lila said. "And we're coming along."

Jessica's heart sank. Why was it that *she* was the one who always got pushed into talking to a boy? But Lila was already standing up, so Jessica had to get up too. She walked across the crowded room with Lila and Ellen at her heels. When she approached Todd's table, she slowed down and smiled.

"Hi, Todd," she said.

"Hi," Todd replied. He looked a little uncertain. "Uh, just leaving?"

"Actually," Jessica said breezily, "we thought we'd see if you wanted some company." She gave a pointed look at the empty chairs at the table.

Todd looked at the other boys, then he looked back at Jessica. "I guess," he said. "Sure. Sit down, if you want to."

Feeling relieved, Jessica took the chair next to Todd's. Lila and Ellen sat down too. After that, things got easier, because there were a lot of things to talk about. They talked about the after-school basketball games, and the school play, and their friends. Then Rick happened to mention the new bowling alley.

"I *love* bowling," Lila blurted excitedly. She turned to Jessica and Ellen. "Don't you love bowling, too?"

"Yes!" Jessica and Ellen chorused. And Jessica added smugly, "I'm pretty good at it, too."

"You are?" Todd asked, glancing at her. "What about your sister?"

Jessica frowned. Why did Todd always want

to know about Elizabeth? "Sure, she bowls," she said with a shrug.

"Somehow, I kind of got the idea that she didn't like it a lot," Todd said thoughtfully.

"We've been talking about going some night," Jessica said.

Todd turned to Rick. "Hey, Rick, want to go bowling some night?"

Lila leaned forward. "That would be great," she said enthusiastically. "Do you like to bowl, Jake?"

"Sure," Jake said. "I was planning to go on Friday night." He turned to Todd and Rick. "Do you guys want to go bowling Friday night?"

Todd cast a quick glance at Jessica. "What night were you and . . . What night were you thinking about?"

Lila's eyes glinted. "Yes, Jessica, what night were you thinking about?"

Jessica smiled in blissful happiness. This couldn't have happened better if she'd planned it. Todd had come right out and asked her for a date, in front of Lila and Ellen! "Friday's fine," she said quickly, before he could change his mind. "Is Friday OK with you?" she asked Lila and Ellen.

"Friday's good for me," Lila said, and Ellen agreed.

"Well, now that's settled," Lila said, "I guess we'd better be going. So we'll see you all on Friday night, at the bowling alley. OK?"

The boys exchanged glances. Jessica noticed that Jake was frowning a little, and Rick looked as if he weren't sure what had happened. Todd cleared his throat. "Yeah," he said, "I guess we'll be there."

"Good," Lila said triumphantly, and the girls left. Out in the mall, where the boys couldn't hear them, they all screamed.

"Jessica, I have to hand it to you," Lila said, "you did that just right."

"A date with Rick Hunter!" Ellen exclaimed, doing a little dance step. "I can hardly believe it!"

"A *triple* date," Lila reminded her. "You and Rick, Jessica and Todd, and . . ." She sighed and closed her eyes. "Jake and me," she added in a dreamy voice.

Jessica frowned. She was remembering Todd's question about Elizabeth. Why had he brought her up? And why had the boys exchanged those glances? Thinking about it, she wasn't sure that Todd had seemed all that excited about their date.

But her frown turned to a smile when Lila and Ellen linked arms with her and began to talk about what they were going to wear on their very first triple date, on Friday night at the bowling alley. To celebrate, Lila invited them all over for dinner at her house that night. That way, they could immediately call Janet and tell her the good news.

Jessica didn't get home from Lila's until nearly nine o'clock. When she did, Elizabeth was in the kitchen talking to her mother.

"Hi, Mom. Hi, Elizabeth," Jessica said, heading for the refrigerator.

"I thought you had dinner at Lila's," Mrs. Wakefield said.

"I did," Jessica replied. She took a couple of slices of cheese and an apple from the refrigerator. "But I'm still hungry."

"I thought you didn't have any appetite anymore," Elizabeth said.

"Oh, that," Jessica replied, dismissing it airily. "That was just a phase. You should have been with us, Elizabeth," she continued. "We had such *fun!*"

"You and Lila?" Mrs. Wakefield asked.

"No, Todd and me," Jessica said dreamily. She nibbled on her cheese. "And Lila and Jake and Ellen and Rick. We all went to Casey's for ice cream."

"And then you had dinner, and now you're

eating more?" Mrs. Wakefield said. "All this talk about food is making me full. I'm going upstairs to do a little work, girls."

Once Mrs. Wakefield had left the kitchen, Jessica turned to her twin. "Guess what, Elizabeth?" she asked. "Todd and I are going bowling on Friday night. *Everybody's* going."

Elizabeth glared at her twin. "Jessica, I thought you were going bowling with me on Friday night."

Jessica frowned. She'd forgotten all about that. "You can come, too, Elizabeth. Not with Todd and me, of course. But I think you should go. Everybody's going to be there."

"You think I should go so I can find a boyfriend, you mean?"

Jessica shifted uncomfortably.

"Maybe I ought to borrow your new denim miniskirt and curl my hair and wear makeup," Elizabeth went on, her eyes blazing. She leaned forward. "Would that improve my chances of getting a boyfriend?"

Jessica took a step backward. "I don't know what you're talking about, Elizabeth."

"Oh yes, you do, Jessica Wakefield!" Elizabeth shouted. "You know exactly what I'm talking about. You and the Unicorns are spreading the rumor that I dressed up on Monday because I wanted to find a boyfriend. Isn't that true?"

Jessica bit her lip. "It wasn't a rumor, Lizzie," she said plaintively. "It was a joke. We didn't mean to—"

"I don't care what you meant!" Elizabeth exclaimed. "It's not a very funny joke. You've humiliated me in front of everybody, and you've made people believe something that isn't true! It was your idea for me to wear makeup and borrow your clothes for school."

"I'm sorry, Elizabeth," Jessica said. "I wouldn't have done it if I thought you'd be hurt. But you had been asking me about boys, and you wanted a different hairstyle. Besides, you told me you liked somebody but you wouldn't tell me who."

"It's none of your business who I like!" Elizabeth said furiously, her fists clenched. "Tell those Unicorns to stop spreading rumors about me." She leaned forward, her blue-green eyes flashing with anger. "Or I'm never speaking to you again!" She stormed out of the room, leaving Jessica staring after her in shock.

Eight

◇

Thursday morning Elizabeth felt better because she had told Jessica exactly how she felt about the rumor. She smiled, remembering Jessica's apology. She knew her twin must have felt really terrible because she had offered to do Elizabeth's chores for the next two days.

But in spite of that, Elizabeth knew that the rumor wasn't going to go away. She knew that people were talking about her. Even putting her hair back into its usual ponytail didn't seem to do any good. It was already too late. All of the sixth-grade boys at Sweet Valley Middle School seemed to believe that she was looking for a boyfriend, and they were all eager to volunteer.

Elizabeth was settling into her homeroom seat

that morning when Colin Harmon approached her.

"Hi, Elizabeth," he said, sitting down on top of the desk in front of her. "Have you heard about the bowling party at the mall tomorrow night?"

Elizabeth rummaged through her backpack, pretending to search for something. She knew that Colin must have heard the rumor and she didn't want him to think she was encouraging him.

"Jessica told me that she's going with some friends," she said. "I didn't know there was going to be a party."

"Well, everybody's going to be there," Colin said. "Including me." He grinned at her. "How about you, Elizabeth? Are you going?"

"I don't think so," Elizabeth said. "I think I have something else to do tomorrow night, with my family."

Colin leaned forward. "You should come bowling. It would be a lot of fun. You and I could team up against some of the other kids."

"I really don't bowl well," Elizabeth said. "I always roll the balls into the gutter. Honestly, Colin, you wouldn't want me on your team."

"I'm a good teacher," Colin persisted, sounding very sure of himself. "I can help you bowl a lot better. In fact, when I get through with you, you'll be an expert." He leaned forward, smiling warmly. "How about it, Elizabeth?"

Elizabeth took a deep breath. Colin obviously wasn't easy to discourage. The only way to deal with him was just to tell him straight out that she wasn't interested.

"Colin," she said as politely as she could, "thanks very much for asking, but I'm not interested in going bowling with you."

Colin looked completely taken aback. He was about to say something when Mr. Davis rapped on his desk and told the students to take their seats. Elizabeth had never been so glad for homeroom to begin. As long as Mr. Davis was reading the announcements, Colin couldn't bother her.

But when she got to English, she couldn't believe what happened. The class was working in groups on oral presentations and, as luck would have it, she and Winston Egbert were grouped together. Ordinarily, it would have been fun for Elizabeth. She liked English and she liked Winston, but today he was acting unbelievably silly.

"Er, ah, Elizabeth," he said, when they were settling down to work, "what would you think if we, ah . . ." His voice trailed off and his ears turned pink. He didn't look at her.

"If we what, Winston?" Elizabeth asked, leafing through her notes.

Winston chewed on his pencil. "If we, well, started this project by, ah . . ."

"By doing what, Winston?" Elizabeth asked, a little impatiently.

Winston's ears got pinker. "Bowling," he muttered.

Elizabeth sighed. So Winston had gotten the word, too. "But bowling doesn't have anything to do with our project," she said.

Winston blinked. "I wasn't talking about our project," he said.

"But that's what we're supposed to be talking about," Elizabeth said firmly. She didn't want to have to tell Winston that she wasn't going bowling on Friday night.

"Oh," Winston replied. His ears turned from pink to red. "Well, OK," he said finally, and they got down to work.

As if Colin Harmon and Winston Egbert didn't present enough problems for Elizabeth to handle, there was Randy Mason, too. Randy was one of the smartest boys in sixth grade, and even though he was terribly shy, he had won the last election for class president. Elizabeth had voted for him and she liked him very much as a friend, so she felt terrible when she turned around from her locker to find him walking bashfully toward her.

"Hi, Elizabeth," he said, pausing beside her. He swallowed. "Uh, how are you?"

"I'm OK," Elizabeth said. Feeling panicky, she started to reach for her books. It wasn't that she didn't want to talk to Randy. It was just that she didn't want to learn that he, like the others, had heard the rumor and believed it. "Listen, I'm in kind of a hurry," she said. "I hope you won't mind if I—"

"Oh, I don't want to keep you," Randy said, his eyes avoiding hers. He reached in his pocket. "I just . . . er, wanted you to have . . . uh, this." He thrust a small gift-wrapped package into her hand.

Elizabeth stared at it. *Oh, no!* she thought. *It's a present! If I accept it, Randy's going to think I'm agreeing to be his girlfriend!* She was about to make an excuse and give it back, when she realized that of course she couldn't do that, either. If she gave the present back, Randy would feel embarrassed for having given it to her in the first place. And that would be even worse. What a terrible fix to be in!

Reluctantly, Elizabeth opened the package. It was a blue-and-green plastic bracelet.

"I hope you like it," he said, shifting from one foot to the other. "It's the color of the dress you wore on Monday," he added with a shy smile. "I mean, I know it's not your birthday or anything, but I thought you might like to have it."

"It's very pretty," Elizabeth said. "Thank you, Randy." She couldn't help wishing that he hadn't given it to her.

Just at that moment, Todd walked by.

"Hi, Elizabeth," he said. He glanced down at the bracelet she held in her hand, and then up at Randy. "Hi, Randy."

"Hi, Todd," Elizabeth and Randy said in unison. Elizabeth felt her cheeks flaming. For a second, she closed her eyes, wanting to cry. Todd must have heard the rumor that she was looking for a boyfriend, and he had just seen her accepting a present from a boy. He would never like her now.

That afternoon, Elizabeth and Amy were walking home from school together. Elizabeth had just told Amy about what happened that day with

Colin, Winston, and Randy, leaving out the part about Todd.

When Elizabeth showed her the plastic bracelet Randy had given her, Amy shook her head and said, "Oh, Elizabeth, you must have felt just awful! And Randy Mason is so nice, too."

"I did feel awful," Elizabeth said sadly. "I still do. I hated to take the bracelet, but I couldn't give it back. I didn't want to hurt Randy's feelings."

"What about Colin Harmon?" Amy asked. "Do you think you hurt his feelings?"

Elizabeth laughed. "I don't mind hurting Colin's feelings. He thinks every girl likes him."

"He is kind of conceited," Amy agreed. "I wish I could have seen his face when you told him that you weren't going bowling with him. But you're going tomorrow night, aren't you, Elizabeth? Everyone's going." She smiled with anticipation. "Even Ken."

Elizabeth shook her head. "No, I've decided to stay home and read. I just don't want to face all those boys, each thinking I might be interested in him." She didn't want to risk running into Todd, either, after what had happened today.

Amy put her hand on Elizabeth's arm. "Elizabeth, you can't stay home!" she exclaimed frantically. "You have to go bowling! You just have to!"

"I do?" Elizabeth asked. "Why?"

"Because if you don't go," Amy replied, "I won't have anybody to talk to."

"But what about Ken?" Elizabeth asked, feeling a little confused. "I thought you were going because you wanted to talk to him."

"I can't talk to Ken all night," Amy replied. "You *have* to come, Elizabeth."

Elizabeth sighed. She really didn't want to go to the bowling alley and spend the night talking to Colin or Winston or Randy. She was hoping that by Monday the Unicorns' rumor would be forgotten, and she could pretend it had never happened. But she didn't want to let Amy down.

"Oh, all right, Amy," she said finally. "I'll go."

Amy gave her a big hug. "Thanks, Elizabeth," she said. "You're a great friend and you won't be sorry."

Later that afternoon Elizabeth was helping her mother carry groceries from the van into the house when a pretty girl strolled up the driveway. She had long black hair, dark eyes, and a creamy complexion. When she spoke, she had a strong Southern accent.

"Hello, Mrs. Wakefield," she said. "We've

never met, but your son has told me a lot about you. My name is Candice. Is Stevie home from school yet?"

If Mrs. Wakefield was surprised to hear Steven's new nickname, she didn't show it. "No, he isn't," she said pleasantly, handing Elizabeth the last bag of groceries. "But I'm sure he'll be along shortly. Would you like to come in and wait?"

Candice gave her a charming smile. "Why, yes, I would," she said. "Thank you so much." She turned to Elizabeth.

"Why, hello there. We met the other day, didn't we, at Casey's Place?"

Elizabeth smiled. "I don't think so. You must have met my sister, Jessica. I'm Elizabeth."

"You two look exactly alike. You must be identical twins. That's so interesting. Stevie didn't tell me he had twin sisters." She pushed a strand of dark hair off of her forehead. "That bag looks a little heavy for you. Why don't you let me carry it?" Before Elizabeth could say a word, Candice had taken the bag out of her arms.

Now Mrs. Wakefield did look surprised. "How nice of you, Candice," she said. When Candice put the bag down on the kitchen counter, Mrs. Wakefield offered her some lemonade.

"That would be lovely," Candice said. She sat

down at the table and sipped her drink, chatting about things that were going on at school. Elizabeth noticed that Steven's name appeared in every other sentence.

Her mother must have noticed it, too. "You and Steven must be good friends," she remarked, after Candice had mentioned Steven for the third or fourth time.

Candice nodded eagerly, her eyes bright. "Oh, we *are*," she said. "Did he tell you that he's taking me to the movies on Saturday night?"

Mrs. Wakefield smiled. "I think he did say something about it," she said. "What movie are you going to see?"

But before Candice could answer, the front door slammed. "Hi, Mom, I'm home," Steven called.

"In here, Steven," his mother answered, going to the refrigerator. "Elizabeth and I are talking to a friend of yours."

"A friend?" Steven replied from the hall. When he came to the kitchen door, there was a look of pleased anticipation on his face, and Elizabeth had the sudden feeling that Steven hoped that the friend was Lindsay. But when he saw Candice sitting at the table, his smile disappeared.

"Hi, Stevie," Candice said brightly.

"Hi, Candice," he said.

Mrs. Wakefield turned from the refrigerator with a jar of spaghetti sauce in her hand. "Candice, I'm fixing spaghetti for dinner tonight," she said. "Would you like to stay?"

Candice jumped up. "That's very nice of you, Mrs. Wakefield," she said. "I'll just go and phone my mother and tell her that you've asked."

When she had left the room, Mrs. Wakefield turned to Steven. "Is that OK with you, Steven?"

Steven heaved a huge sigh. "Yeah, Mom," he said. "It's fine."

But everything wasn't fine, Elizabeth could see. Although Candice was a very nice girl, Elizabeth knew that Steven was more interested in Lindsay and he didn't know what to do about Candice's attention.

At dinner, Steven hardly spoke. He just sat at the table shoveling his spaghetti away in big bites. As soon as the meal was over, he jumped up and said, "Come on, Candice, I'll walk you home."

"There's seconds on apple pie," Mrs. Wakefield said. "Don't you want another piece, Steven?"

"No, thanks," Steven said emphatically. "I'm full."

Mrs. Wakefield looked surprised, and Elizabeth and Jessica traded glances. Steven *never* turned down seconds on homemade apple pie.

"How about you, Candice?" Mrs. Wakefield asked politely. "Another piece?"

Candice looked at Steven, who was already standing up. Then she put down her napkin and said, "No, thank you. I guess I'd better be going."

Mr. Wakefield smiled. "Don't forget, you have some chores to do when you come back. And you've got your homework, so don't be too long."

"Oh, I won't," Steven assured him cheerfully. "In fact, I've got tons of homework, so I'll be home in less than ten minutes. Come on, Candice, let's go." He left, practically dragging her out of the room.

Mr. Wakefield shook his head. "What was that all about?" he asked, surprised. "Was it my imagination, or did Steven sound enthusiastic about the prospect of tons of homework?"

"And he turned down a second piece of pie," Mrs. Wakefield marveled. "It must be love."

Jessica laughed. "You're right, Mom, but it doesn't have to do with Candice. Steven has another girlfriend named Lindsay," she explained. "He was trying to get rid of Candice."

"How do you know so much about Steven's love life, Jessica?" Mr. Wakefield asked.

Before Jessica could answer, Mrs. Wakefield said, "But why would he be trying to get rid of her? She's such a nice girl, and they've got a date on Saturday night. Didn't she say that, Elizabeth?" Elizabeth nodded, feeling sorry for Steven.

"He does have a date with her on Saturday night," Jessica replied. "But he's got a date with Lindsay on Friday night, to go bowling. She's the girl he *really* likes."

Mr. Wakefield raised his eyebrows at Mrs. Wakefield as he got up to clear the table. "What do you think, Alice?"

Mrs. Wakefield sighed. "Perhaps I ought to have a word with Steven."

True to his word, Steven was home in ten minutes. Elizabeth and her mother were in the den measuring the windows for new drapes when he came in.

"Steven," Mrs. Wakefield said, "is it true that you have a date with Lindsay on Friday night and a date with Candice on Saturday night?"

Steven looked at the floor. "Yes," he muttered. "It's true."

"Does Candice know that you're seeing Lindsay?" Mrs. Wakefield went on.

Steven shook his head.

"Does Lindsay know that you're seeing Candice?"

Steven shook his head again.

"I'm surprised at you, Steven. You're not being fair to either girl. It's OK to date more than one girl if you're honest with each of them. But you shouldn't sneak around. And if you don't really like one of them, you shouldn't continue to encourage her."

"But I haven't encouraged her," Steven said desperately. "I mean, I'm not encouraging her now." He stopped. "I mean, I thought for a while that I liked her a lot. Then I decided I liked Lindsay more. But by that time, Candice had gotten the idea that she and I . . . I mean, that I was going to . . ." He stopped, looking frustrated and unhappy. "I wish I knew what to do about her."

"I'm sure you'll figure something out, Steven," Mrs. Wakefield said. She turned back to the window to continue her measuring as Steven left the room.

Elizabeth couldn't remember ever seeing him look more miserable.

Nine

◇

After finishing her homework, Elizabeth went down to the kitchen to make some hot chocolate. She found Steven sitting at the table with his head in his hands.

"Hi, Steven," Elizabeth said. She poured some milk into a cup and put it in the microwave. "I'm making some hot chocolate. Would you like me to make you some, too?"

Steven sighed. "Sure," he said. "That would be great."

There was a long silence as Elizabeth added some chocolate to the hot milk and stirred it. She carried the steaming cup to Steven and placed it in front of him.

Steven put his hands around the cup. Then

he cleared his throat. "Elizabeth," he said, without looking up, "you usually have good ideas about people. What would you do if you were . . . well, in my situation?"

Elizabeth sat down at the table across from Steven. Normally, Steven never asked for advice from anyone, least of all from his little sisters. But she suspected that he might not want to talk to any of his friends about Candice and Lindsay. Anyway, it sounded as if he genuinely wanted her opinion.

She thought for a moment. What would she do if she had two boyfriends, one she liked and one she'd like to get rid of? Elizabeth smiled, remembering how awkward she felt when Randy was giving her the bracelet and Todd walked past and saw them. It was funny, but she had a problem almost like the one Steven had.

"If it were my problem, Steven," she said softly, "and I really wanted to keep Lindsay's friendship, I'd be honest with Candice."

"How can I tell her how I really feel?" he asked, looking up. "You saw what she's like. She really thinks I like her."

"That's why you have to tell her the truth." Elizabeth sipped her hot chocolate. "If Candice doesn't know exactly how you feel, she could keep fooling herself for weeks and weeks."

Steven put down his cup and frowned. "That means that she could keep hanging around for weeks and weeks, too—which could be pretty embarrassing."

Elizabeth nodded. "It could be worse than embarrassing," she observed. "If Lindsay finds out that Candice is hanging around, she might get the idea that you're encouraging her. She might think you like her."

"But what can I say?"

"Just tell her the truth, Steven—that you like her as a friend, but that's as far as it goes."

"It sounds simple enough when you say it, Elizabeth," Steven replied. "But believe me, telling Candice that I like her as a friend is not going to be easy. It's not something I'm looking forward to." His shoulders slumped. "But I guess I don't have any choice, do I?"

He drained his hot chocolate and stood up. "Thanks, Liz," he said, looking down at her. "I appreciate the advice."

Steven was on his way out of the kitchen when Jessica barged into the room.

"Hi, Stevie," Jessica purred, in a perfect imitation of Candice. "Did we have fun tonight?"

Steven glared at her, then stomped out of the kitchen without a word.

Jessica and Ellen were going over to Lila's house to get ready for the bowling party. Jessica spent an hour rummaging through her closet and drawers, trying things on and looking at herself in the mirror. Should she wear her yellow top and her short denim skirt, with yellow socks and high tops? Or maybe her white jeans and a black turtleneck? Or her pink-and-white striped T-shirt and a short white pleated skirt, with pink sneakers and pink socks? In the end, she couldn't make up her mind, so she put all three outfits into a duffel bag. She was zipping it when Ellen arrived to pick her up.

Ellen glanced at the duffel bag. "I didn't know you were going to stay at Lila's for the weekend," she said, looking surprised.

"I'm not," Jessica said. "I just can't decide what to wear. I thought maybe you and Lila could help me."

When Jessica and Ellen got to Lila's house, Jessica spent another hour trying on her three outfits so her friends could tell her which looked cuter. They finally decided that she should wear the pink outfit, and Lila decided she would wear her new designer jeans and green top. While Lila got dressed and Ellen put on makeup and Jessica curled her hair, they talked about Jake and Rick and Todd.

"Rick walked me to social studies class this afternoon," Ellen reported, "and he said for sure that he's going to be there tonight."

"Janet said that Jake told her he's going, too," Lila said, running a brush through her brown hair. "Janet is planning to get there early, so she's saving us a lane."

"But I thought we were going to get a lane with the boys," Jessica objected. She added a touch of pink gloss to her lips.

Even though they'd been talking about going bowling for two days and had told all the other Unicorns about their plans, Jessica was still a little uncertain about it. After all, Todd hadn't said a word about going bowling together when she had "accidentally" bumped into him in front of his locker that afternoon.

Lila busied herself with her hairbrush. "We don't know for sure what will happen until we get there," she replied. "Anyway, the bowling alley will probably be crowded. It's better to have Janet save us a lane than not to have one at all, don't you think?"

Jessica and Ellen agreed that Lila was right. When they had finished dressing, Mr. Fowler gave them a ride to the mall.

The bowling alley was crowded, and the air was filled with the rumble of bowling balls and the clatter of falling pins. It seemed to Jessica that everybody from Sweet Valley Middle School was there, and she saw several of Steven's friends from Sweet Valley High, as well. The three girls had been hoping that they would immediately bump into the boys and find a lane together, but they were disappointed at what they found. Already, the middle-school gang had split into two crowds, the girls' crowd and the boys' crowd. The boys, including Rick, Jake, and Todd, were bowling together in their lanes. The girls were sticking to theirs.

"Hi, Lila, Jessica, Ellen—over here." Jessica spotted Janet Howell waving at them from a lane right next to seventh grader Bruce Patman and some of his friends. Lila wasn't especially fond of Bruce because the Fowlers and the Patmans were rivals in Sweet Valley, but all the other Unicorns thought he was extremely cute. So Jessica and Ellen, with Lila grumbling behind, went hurrying over to join Janet and the other Unicorns.

"Jake is over there, Lila," Janet said, pointing. "In the second lane."

Lila tossed her long hair behind her shoulders. "I see him," she said.

"Well?" Janet wanted to know.

Lila looked at her. "Well, what?"

Janet smiled a little. "I thought you had a date."

"We told the boys we'd see them here," Ellen explained hurriedly. "We'll talk to them later. Maybe we'll get a lane together then."

Janet nodded. "I've been saving room here, if you want to bowl with us," she said.

Jessica looked toward the next lane to see Bruce Patman waving at her. Beside him, Aaron Dallas ran his hand through his brown hair and gave her a grin.

"Thanks for saving room, Janet," Jessica said, smiling back at Aaron. She saw that he had a dimple in his right cheek that flashed when he smiled. It was funny that she'd never noticed it before. "We'd love to bowl with you."

Beside Aaron, Tom Sleeter grinned at Ellen.

"Yes, we'd love to," Ellen told Janet.

"Well, why don't you go first, then, Lila," Janet said, marking her down on the score card.

As Lila was choosing her ball, Aaron walked

over and leaned on the divider between the two lanes. "Are you going to show us how many strikes you can throw, Jessica?" he asked.

Jessica smiled at him. "Maybe," she said.

Lila's first ball knocked down two pins. Her second ball knocked down three more.

"Your turn, Jessica," Janet announced after she'd marked down Lila's score.

Jessica took her ball and went to the line. Next to her, Aaron was bowling, too. Her first ball knocked down seven pins, leaving three standing on one side.

"Hey, that's good, Jessica!" Ellen called out. "Now all you have to do is get those three!"

Next to Jessica, Aaron had narrowed his eyes in concentration. He took careful aim and threw the ball, his first. Five pins went down, leaving five still standing.

"Look, everybody," Janet crowed delightedly. "Jessica got more than Aaron!"

Aaron frowned. "I always do better with the second ball," he muttered.

Jessica reached for her ball. Aaron was still frowning. She took several steps, then threw the ball and watched as it rolled directly toward the last three pins.

"Yay, Jess!" Ellen cried. "Great job."

Jessica glanced at Aaron. He didn't look as if he thought it was so great.

He picked up his ball, wiped one hand and then the other on his pants, settled into position, and threw the ball. It wobbled down one side of the lane. At the last moment, while Jessica held her breath, it curved in and banged into the five pins. Four of them crashed to the floor while the fifth one teetered back and forth. At last, it fell down, too. Jessica let out her breath.

"See?" Aaron said, dusting his hands. He grinned at her. "My secret is in the second ball."

Jessica smiled at him. "I see," she said. "You're a good bowler, Aaron."

Aaron's grin got bigger. "Hey, Jessica, would you like a soda?" he asked.

"That would be nice," Jessica said. With a wave to Lila, Ellen, Janet, and the rest of the Unicorns, she joined Aaron.

As Jessica and Aaron made their way toward the snack bar, Elizabeth and Amy walked in. They were accompanied by Julie Porter, whom they had met in the parking lot. After a lot of thought, Elizabeth had decided to wear her hair down. It was the way *she* liked it, and that was the way it was going to be. If the other kids wanted to make something of it, let them.

"Hey, Elizabeth," Amy said, looking around, "I wonder what happened to all the big dates Jessica's been telling you about?"

"Yeah, it doesn't look to me like anybody's on a date here," Julie said.

No one was paired off. Instead, there was a lot of giggling, running back and forth between the lanes, and dashing to the soft drink stand. Elizabeth noticed that the Unicorns were bowling next to Bruce Patman, Tom Sleeter, and some other boys. She glanced around, noticing to her relief that Randy Mason, Colin Harmon, and Winston Egbert were down at the far end of the alley, almost out of sight. But where was Todd? Why weren't he and Jessica bowling together?

Amy grabbed Elizabeth's arm and pointed. "Look," she said excitedly. "There's Ken, over there, in the fourth lane, with Todd Wilkins and Tom McKay. And the lane next to them is empty. Come on, let's go!"

Elizabeth followed Amy and Julie to sign up for the lane. A few minutes later, the girls were settling down in the lane next to the boys.

Even though she was very conscious of Todd's presence, Elizabeth had plenty to do to keep busy for the first several minutes. She set up the score-card for Amy and Julie and herself, and scored Amy's and Julie's throws.

Then Todd leaned over and spoke to her. "Hi." He grinned. "So you decided to come after all, huh?"

Elizabeth nodded wordlessly, feeling very shy. She wondered if he was thinking about what he had seen in the hallway between her and Randy. Or maybe he was thinking of the rumor the Unicorns had spread around. Suddenly she wished she hadn't come at all.

Tom McKay spoke up. "Hey," he said, grinning, "why don't we have a competition? The boys against the girls?"

"That would be fun," Amy and Julie agreed, and Elizabeth had to say yes.

"OK, then," Tom said. He turned to Todd. "Todd, it's your turn. Show them what you can do."

Todd stepped up to the line. Quickly, he threw two balls, and scored an eight overall, leaving two pins still standing.

Todd turned to Elizabeth. "You're next."

Elizabeth's hands felt very cold and clammy. She shook them nervously, then picked up a ball. She could feel Todd's eyes on her.

"Come on," Amy called encouragingly, "let's see a strike! We want to beat these guys."

Elizabeth couldn't help laughing. "If I bowl a strike," she said, "it'll be the first one in my whole life."

"There's a first time for everything," Julie reminded her. "Come on, we want to *win!*"

Elizabeth stepped back, took two running steps, and threw the ball. To her enormous surprise, it went straight down the middle of the lane and smashed into the pins. Every single one of them crashed to the floor.

"A *strike!*" Amy yelled, jumping up and down. "I knew you could do it! Now we're ahead!"

"Hey," Todd said admiringly, "that was pretty good."

"Thanks," Elizabeth said, smiling at him. She didn't feel quite so self-conscious now. As she went back to keeping score for the girls and laughing and joking with Todd and the other boys, she realized that she was having a lot of fun. She was bowling very well, too, better than ever before. She wasn't the high scorer, but she was close to the top.

For Elizabeth, the whole evening had taken on a wonderful sparkle—until a brand-new thought suddenly struck her. Todd hadn't mentioned her name, not even once. And as far as she could remember, her friends hadn't called her by name, either. Was it possible that Todd had mistaken her for Jessica? After all, she had told him the other day that she wasn't a good bowler. He wouldn't believe that it was *Elizabeth* who had bowled that perfect strike. Elizabeth also knew he and Jessica were supposed to be having a date tonight. Did he think that she was Jessica?

The thought made Elizabeth's stomach knot up. She had to make certain that Todd really knew who she was. But at the same time, she didn't want to let him know. She had been having such a good time. It would be awful if Todd went off to look for Jessica when he discovered his mistake.

Elizabeth was still thinking about her problem when Amy nudged her. "Hey," she said, "your brother's here."

Elizabeth looked up. Steven and Lindsay were just joining some other kids from Sweet Valley High in the lane on the other side of them. Steven had his arm around Lindsay's shoulder, and he looked relaxed and happy—much more relaxed and happy than she'd seen him looking at home lately.

Then suddenly, Steven's face changed. His

jaw tightened and he turned bright red. Elizabeth turned to see what Steven was looking at.

It was Candice. She was coming toward him through the crowd. And from the look on her face, Elizabeth knew that Steven was in for trouble.

Ten

◇

Elizabeth stared as Candice charged up to Steven. "I thought you had to do something with your family tonight," she said, her hands on her hips. She turned to Lindsay, looking her up and down. "Some family!" she yelled. "I suppose this is another sister—one I haven't met yet."

"Uh, hi, er, Candice," Steven stammered helplessly. He turned with a sick smile to Lindsay. "Uh, Lindsay, have you and Candice met?"

Lindsay spoke with dignity. "I don't think so," she said in a rather distant voice. "But maybe we should."

"Yes," Candice said in a mocking tone. "Maybe we should. We might discover that we have something in common. Isn't that right, Stevie?"

Elizabeth clenched her hands, silently rooting for Steven. *Come on, Steven,* she thought urgently. *Don't let Candice bully you this way.*

Suddenly, Steven seemed to pull himself together. "Excuse me," he said to Lindsay. "Go ahead and start bowling without me. I need to speak to Candice for a minute."

Steven took Candice firmly by the arm and steered her through the crowd to the corner by the drinking fountain. They were too far away for Elizabeth to hear what Steven was saying to her, but she could see that he had a firm look on his face and was speaking very seriously. At first, Candice still looked very angry, but then she began to pout. When it was all over, she walked away, looking downcast, and Steven returned to the lane. He sat down next to Lindsay and began to talk to her in a low voice.

Elizabeth almost jumped up and cheered when she saw Lindsay lean over and kiss Steven on the cheek. Obviously, Steven's romantic crisis was over.

Amy nudged Elizabeth again. "Everybody's taking a break," she said. "Julie and Tom have gone to talk to some of Tom's friends. Ken has gone over to the refreshment stand. Now's my chance to talk to him."

"Good luck," Elizabeth said. She looked around but she didn't see Todd anywhere. Maybe he had realized that he had made a mistake and had gone off to look for Jessica.

"You have to come, too, Elizabeth!" Amy exclaimed. "I can't go by myself. What if Ken doesn't want to talk to me?"

Elizabeth sighed and pushed the thought of Todd out of her mind. "Amy," she pointed out, "Ken has been bowling beside you for the last half hour, and the two of you have been having a great time together. Besides, you're friends. Why wouldn't he want to talk to you?"

"Please come," Amy begged. "I know I'm being silly, but I feel funny, and I don't want to go all by myself."

Elizabeth followed Amy to the refreshment stand, where Amy got a hot dog and Elizabeth got a soda. Then they wandered over to where Ken was sitting on a stool, eating a slice of pizza.

Ken looked up. "Hi, Amy. Hi, Elizabeth," he said. He pointed to the stool beside him. "Want to sit down?"

"Hi, Ken," Amy exclaimed. "I'd love to." She sat down and they immediately began talking about the last game. Elizabeth was just heading back to her lane when she saw Steven.

"Hi, Elizabeth," Steven said. He was carrying a tray with two hot dogs and two sodas. "Hey, you know, for a little sister you give some pretty good advice," he said. "Candice showed up a little while ago."

"I know," Elizabeth told him. "I saw her. She looked a little upset."

"That's the understatement of the year," Steven said. "But it came out OK. I told her what you said—that I liked her as a friend, but nothing more."

"How did she take it?" Elizabeth asked.

Steven shrugged. "She was upset at first. But she'll get over it. In fact, I caught a glimpse of her a minute ago. She was bowling with Sam Morse, so I don't think her heart is broken."

Elizabeth sipped her drink. "Is Lindsay feeling OK about everything?"

Steven nodded. "I think she was happy that I was straight with her about it."

"That's good," Elizabeth said. "I'm glad that everything turned out OK for you."

Steven shifted from one foot to the other. "Uh, Elizabeth," he said, looking at the floor, "I probably haven't told you this before. But it's actually not so bad, having you for a sister."

"Thanks, Steven," Elizabeth replied. It was

probably the nicest thing that her brother had ever said to her. She watched him as he rejoined Lindsay.

Then, since she had nothing better to do, she wandered over to the jukebox and stood in front of it, thinking about how much had changed in the past few months. Although they had had a few problems in the past week, she and Jessica were closer than ever. Steven was behaving more like a real brother and less like an arrogant know-it-all, and he'd straightened out his tangled relationship with Candice and Lindsay. Everybody else seemed to be getting together, too. There were Amy and Ken, Jessica and Todd, Julie and Tom. And even though things hadn't worked out between her and Todd, Elizabeth was beginning to enjoy being around boys.

She fished in her pocket and pulled out some change. One of her favorite Darcy Campman songs was on the jukebox—a soft, wistful ballad called "Getting Together." She dropped the coins into the slot and waited while the machine clicked and whirred and the music began to play.

Elizabeth suddenly became aware that somebody was standing beside her. She turned her head and saw that it was Todd. To her surprise, he was alone. Where was Jessica?

Todd didn't speak for a moment and they just stood, silently, listening to the music. Finally, he said, "Did you put this song on?"

Elizabeth nodded. "It's one of my favorites." She wanted to ask where Jessica was, and why they weren't together, but she didn't.

"Mine, too," he said. "I love Darcy Campman. I like your hair that way," he added shyly. "It looks nice."

"Thanks," Elizabeth said, suddenly feeling awful. Obviously, Todd was still confused. He thought she was Jessica. It was tempting to play along with his mistake, because it was nice to be with him. But Elizabeth couldn't do that any longer.

"Todd," she said, taking a deep breath, "there's something I have to tell you."

"Yeah?" Todd asked, sounding interested. He stuck his hands in his pockets. "What is it?"

Elizabeth shifted nervously. "I, uh, that is . . ." She swallowed. "I'm not who you think I am. You . . . you've got the wrong twin."

Todd grinned. "No, I haven't," he said. "For once, I've got the right one."

"But I'm Elizabeth," Elizabeth protested. "It's *Jessica* you're supposed to have a date with tonight."

Todd frowned. "I was afraid you'd heard that

rumor, Elizabeth," he muttered. "I just wish I knew who started it."

"Rumor?" Elizabeth asked. She could feel herself getting red. Todd must be talking about the rumor the Unicorns had started about her. She sighed, wishing he hadn't brought it up. "I guess you mean the one about—" she began.

"The one about me and your sister," Todd said. He flushed, looking embarrassed. "I ran into Jessica at Casey's one day after school, and I'm afraid I let her get the idea that we were going to be together tonight. But I didn't mean it that way, Elizabeth. I just meant that I was planning to come bowling, that's all. But then, the next day, I heard people saying that Jessica and I were supposed to have a date. It . . ." He paused and swallowed, his face getting even redder. "It bothered me, especially because I . . . well, I suspected that maybe Jessica liked me."

"Oh," Elizabeth said. She managed a shaky little laugh. "Then you didn't have the two of us mixed up?"

"No way." Todd laughed. "At first, at school, when you started wearing your hair that way, I got confused. But I can usually tell you apart."

"Really?" Elizabeth was surprised.

"Uh-huh. You and Jessica are pretty different—in lots of ways. *Important* ways." He smiled. "Hey, the song's over, and I'm in the mood for some ice cream. Want to go over to Casey's Place with me? We can get a couple of milk shakes and talk for a while."

Elizabeth stared at him, astonished. So all along Todd had really liked her.

While they were ordering their milk shakes, Todd explained that he had wanted to ask her to go bowling earlier that week. "But when we talked in front of your locker, I got the feeling that you weren't exactly crazy about bowling, so I didn't say anything."

Elizabeth laughed. "That was a pretty awful conversation, wasn't it?"

Todd looked down at his milk shake. "It was pretty uncomfortable," he said. "I couldn't figure out what to say. I knew I was messing up, but I didn't know how to fix it."

Elizabeth stared at him. He thought *he'd* messed up and she thought *she'd* messed up! Somehow, the idea was really comforting.

As they talked, Elizabeth discovered that she and Todd had a lot in common. He liked to read mystery stories, and he also liked horses. Once in a while he'd gone up to Carson Stables, where

Elizabeth rode. He enjoyed bike riding as much as she did.

Todd looked at her. "Hey, maybe you'd like to go bike riding sometime," he suggested.

"That would be great, Todd."

Todd looked down at his milk shake and then back at her with a smile. "Do you think having milk shakes together counts as a date?" he asked.

Elizabeth giggled. "I don't think so," she said. "Do you?"

"Probably not," he agreed. "But people around here seem to like starting rumors."

Elizabeth shifted uncomfortably. "Uh, Todd," she said, "speaking of rumors, there was one going around at school—"

"I know," Todd said. "I heard what the Unicorns were saying about you. But I didn't believe it."

"You didn't?"

"Of course not," he said. "Your sister might do something like that. But you wouldn't." He slurped up the last of his milk shake. "Maybe we'd better get back to the bowling alley," he said, glancing at his watch. "We could look for Ken, Amy, Tom, and Julie and bowl another game."

As they walked back to the bowling alley, Todd held Elizabeth's hand. When he leaned over and gave her a kiss on the cheek, she thought she was the happiest, luckiest girl in Sweet Valley. And then suddenly she remembered something that made her happiness vanish.

She'd forgotten all about Jessica!

Jessica had been having so much fun with Aaron that it hadn't even occurred to her to wonder what sort of evening Elizabeth was having. She was a little surprised when Mary Wallace came up to her and said, "Have you heard about Elizabeth?"

Jessica applauded Aaron's throw. "What about Elizabeth?" she asked distractedly.

Mary sat down beside Jessica. "Maybe you won't like it," she said. Then she glanced at Aaron. "On the other hand, maybe it won't bother you."

Jessica turned to look at Mary. "Maybe *what* won't bother me?"

"That Elizabeth went off with Todd," Mary said, a little uncomfortably. "Kimberly Haver saw them going into Casey's together a while ago."

Aaron came back to Jessica, dusting his hands and looking triumphant. "What did you think about that last ball, Jessica?"

"I thought it was terrific, Aaron," Jessica said

enthusiastically, noticing the cute way the dimple reappeared in Aaron's cheek when he smiled. She smiled at Mary. "Of course it doesn't bother me about Elizabeth and Todd, Mary. Why should it? If they want to go to Casey's together, let them."

"Speaking of Casey's," Aaron put in, "I'm about ready for a milk shake. How about you, Jessica?" He turned to Mary. "Maybe you and Peter would like to join us, Mary."

As Mary nodded and smiled, Jessica jumped up. "What a great idea!" she exclaimed. "The four of us. Let's go!"

The minute Elizabeth thought about Jessica, she began to feel cold inside. Her sister had told everybody that she had a date with Todd tonight. She would be furious when she discovered that Elizabeth had spent the evening bowling with him and then had gone off to Casey's with him, alone.

Elizabeth swallowed hard. What was she going to do? How was she going to break the news to Jessica?

Just then, Todd nudged her. "Hey, Elizabeth," he said. "Look. There's Jessica."

With a sinking feeling in her stomach, Elizabeth looked. Jessica was coming toward them. But she wasn't by herself. She was with Mary Wallace,

Peter Jeffries, and Aaron Dallas. And she and Aaron were hand-in-hand. When she saw that Elizabeth was with Todd, she didn't seem to mind a bit. In fact, she smiled at Todd and Elizabeth and gave them a friendly wave.

Todd looked at Elizabeth and they both burst out laughing.

As Elizabeth slipped into a seat beside Amy and reached for the scorecard, Amy gave her a curious look.

"Where have you been?" she demanded. "After I finished talking to Ken, I looked all over for you."

"You'll never guess," Elizabeth whispered. The first chance she got, she would tell Amy everything.

But before Elizabeth talked to Amy, she wanted to talk to Jessica. That night, when the girls got home from the bowling alley, Jessica came in and flopped down on Elizabeth's bed.

"Wasn't it great?" she asked dreamily. "I've never had so much fun in my whole life."

Elizabeth looked at her twin. "Is it really OK?" she asked. "About Todd and me, I mean?"

Jessica sat up. "Of course it's OK. But that reminds me, Elizabeth. I thought you didn't like

Todd Wilkins," she said accusingly. "That's what you told me, anyway."

Elizabeth sighed and picked up her hairbrush. "I was trying to keep it a secret," she said. "I thought *you* liked him."

"I did," Jessica said, sounding a little defensive. "I just decided that Aaron was cuter, that's all. Anyway," she confided, "I was beginning to think that maybe Todd wasn't all that anxious to be my boyfriend."

"You were?" Elizabeth asked in surprise.

"Yes. Somehow, when we were together, the conversation kept coming around to you." Jessica laughed a little. "I guess I didn't want to think about it at the time. But looking back on it, I'll bet that Todd was more interested in you than me right from the start."

Elizabeth stared at her twin. She hadn't expected Jessica to say such a thing, even if it might be true.

"Anyway," Jessica went on, "everything is just fine. All the Unicorns think that Aaron is absolutely the cutest, and *everybody* saw us together tonight. In fact, there's only one thing that would have made tonight even better."

Elizabeth sat down in front of the mirror and began to brush her hair. "What's that?"

Jessica's tone got even dreamier. "It would have been nice if Aaron had kissed me," she said. "That would make me the first sixth-grade Unicorn to be kissed. If that had happened, Lila and Ellen would turn absolutely green with envy."

Elizabeth stopped brushing her hair. "Want to know something, Jess?" she asked.

Jessica was pulling off her tennis shoes. "What?"

"Todd kissed me."

Jessica dropped her shoe. Her mouth fell open. "He *kissed* you?" she squealed. "Really, truly, Lizzie?"

Elizabeth laughed. "Really, truly, Jess."

Jessica ran over and threw her arms around Elizabeth. "Wow!" she cried. "That's *fantastic*! Your first kiss! Just wait until Lila hears this!"

Elizabeth's eyes widened. "Jessica!" she exclaimed, horrified. "You wouldn't!"

Jessica stared at her. "You mean, you want to keep your first kiss a *secret*?"

"Absolutely," Elizabeth said. "I don't want a soul in the world to know but the two of us. Jessica, if you tell—"

Jessica laughed. "I was just teasing, Elizabeth," she said. "I won't tell anybody. I promise. Nobody will know but you and me—and Todd, of course."

"And Amy," Elizabeth added. "I'm going to tell her, too." She looked at her sister. "It's so great to have a twin!"

"What's even greater is that now we have so much in common," Jessica said. "Now that you're interested in boys, we'll have so much more to talk about! I can talk about Aaron, and you can talk about Todd, and—"

Elizabeth laughed. "I think I've talked enough about boys for one night, Jess."

"Well, *I* haven't," Jessica said, settling back down on the bed. "Just wait until I tell you about the fun I had bowling with Aaron."

Elizabeth shook her head.

On Saturday morning, Mrs. Wakefield drove Elizabeth over to Amy's house. The girls were partners on a science project and they were planning to do a chart on endangered species, complete with photographs. To get started, they asked Mrs. Sutton to drive them to the zoo.

Once Mrs. Sutton had dropped them off, Amy and Elizabeth wandered over to see the new baby gorilla.

"Come on, Elizabeth," Amy said. "I've been waiting to hear about last night."

"Well," Elizabeth began, "it turns out Todd

was never really interested in Jessica after all. And Jessica was never really interested in Todd, either."

"What?" Amy looked confused.

"When you and Ken started talking last night," Elizabeth explained, "Todd asked me to go to Casey's Place with him."

"Really?" Amy asked.

"Uh-huh. I figured out that what Jessica was really interested in was being the first sixth-grade Unicorn to have a boyfriend. Anyway, Jess got together with Aaron Dallas last night. So it all worked out OK."

Amy gave her a sideways glance. "So, Todd was the one all along, huh?"

Elizabeth laughed a little. "Yes. I'm sorry I couldn't tell you. But since I couldn't tell Jess, I didn't think it was right to tell anyone."

"I understand," Amy said. "Anyway, I'm glad it's Todd. I like him."

Elizabeth blushed. "Can I tell you a secret? I mean, a *real* secret. It's something important, that you can't tell *anybody* else."

Amy gave her a curious look. "Of course. You know that I'd never tell anybody about a secret of yours. What is it?"

"Todd kissed me last night."

"Wow, Elizabeth," Amy breathed, sounding awed. "That *is* a real secret!"

Elizabeth laughed. "And now that I've told you, can we please stop talking about boys? Jessica is convinced that since Todd and I got together, all I'll ever want to talk about is boys. I'm glad you're around to talk to me about other things, Amy."

Amy grinned and pointed at the new baby gorilla. "Like endangered species, huh?"

Elizabeth pulled out her camera and got ready to take a picture. "Like endangered species," she said. "And like school, and the *Sixers* and—" She stopped and grinned. "I'm really lucky to have you as a friend, Amy. It's almost like having another sister. I can tell you anything, and I can trust you to keep even my deepest secrets. And I never have to worry about making you mad or hurting your feelings."

Amy nodded solemnly. "I know. I'm glad we're friends, too. For me, it really *is* like having a sister. Nothing will ever come between us!"

What could possibly come between Amy and Elizabeth? Find out in Sweet Valley Twins #44, **AMY MOVES IN.**

Bantam Books in the SWEET VALLEY KIDS series